Nwelezelanga

Nwelezelanga

The Star Child

Unathi Magubeni

First published by Blackbird Books, 2016
Second and third impression 2016
Fourth and fifth impression 2017
Sixth impression 2019
Seventh impression 2020

593 Zone 4
Seshego
Polokwane 0742
South Africa
www.blackbirdbooks.africa

ISBN 978-1-928337-24-9
Also available as an ebook.

Cover artwork © Sindiso Khumalo
Set in Sabon 10/13pt
Printed by ABC Press, Cape Town
Job no. 16410

See a complete list of Blackbird Books titles at
www.blackbirdbooks.africa

Part One

One

I HAVE MANY NAMES; my mother calls me 'Nwelezelanga' because of my golden hair. Some call me 'Mhlophe' because of my fair, almost-ginger skin. One wise old woman of the tribe calls me 'Mehlomadala' because of my big round eyes that reflect oceans of untold stories. The village girls who like to taunt me just call me 'that albino girl'.

I'm thirteen years old; however, that's a distortion on its own. I'm young yet old; I've experienced the cycle of birth and death many more times than I care to count. I've donned and shredded many skin colours in my lifetime. I've lived the lives of many; the lives of the poor and the healers of Bantu and served the divine purpose in countless ways. I have also visited this world before as a baobab tree and stood tall for over a hundred years exuding all the wisdom in the known world. I've made short visits sometimes as a carefree butterfly showing off the innocence from beyond. One of my favourite incarnations was when I was a bird and would cross the oceans with my own kind, reflecting the endurance of the immortals. On occasion, I have visited this world in less glamorous roles such as in the form of a worker bee and worked all my waking life giving the world the sweet honey of my hard labour.

I spend most of my time suspended in the hills of my humble village. I watch the clouds, looking for messages from beyond. I watch them morph into countless symbols speaking the language of the gods. I struggle to decode some of the messages. I have to be patient; there are hidden secrets in the eternal knot of existence. Many think I'm crazy and find my favourite pastime an excuse for being lazy.

'Uhlala njalo ugcakamele amalanga,' they mock, calling me a 'lethargic turd'.

'She is crazy that one,' the village women gossip with their eyes.

'The heavens are not going to fall any time soon,' the young girls my age tease.

They don't know any better; I've tasted immortality and bathed in its deep ancient waters. I've swum aeons on end in the stream of eternal bliss. I have gone beyond all mortal emotions and painted the path in the unknown with colourless light. There are only stories of joy and profound peace in this foreign land; freedom is the essence of our existence in the world of the spirits.

I don't have many friends and am an outcast of sorts; the situation is exacerbated by the fact that I do not attend school. I'm frowned upon by my peers. There is one old woman, Nomkhubulwana, who is my friend. She is kind to me. She's aged yet a dancing spirit of a child lights up her face. She tells me stories of the land; stories of growing up in the village of Dingilizwe. She comes with me up the hill sometimes, picking wild berries along the way. We have many things in common; we were both sent by the great spirit of Qamata to this land of the walking dead to satisfy earthly desires and pass messages from beyond. We have a purpose to serve; a divine responsibility to each one of us, children of the star.

Along the cycle of birth and death, I somehow got tired of the pitiful physical existence and begged the all-knowing one for a permanent residence in the world of the spirits and my wish was granted. I have spent many folds of lifetimes in the land of the holy ones before being born again in this lifetime. All the words and emotions would fall short to describe the profound serenity of the spirit world we call home. I can be silence, light or nothing in a few moments. I can be as carefree as the wind, defying all space and time with no birth in sight; we play games in multidimensional realities. The enlightened ones visit us for a while in the land of the divine before being summoned to earthly missions. We have fun knowing that the call to duty can fall at any moment.

My call came and I was ready to serve; for some strange reason I missed the confined and predictable world of the walking dead. It has its unique charms. The all-knowing one summoned me to listen to the prayers of the woman who would be my mother. She wept as she knelt on top of Mount Ntabankulu.

'Bless me with a child, my lord, and I will be forever grateful,' she cried. 'What is the use of a wife if she can't bear children?'

I felt her pain.

'Grant me just one child, oh all-knowing Qamata, and I promise to give her all my love,' she begged and prayed until her mouth was dry; I was born ten moons later.

The hut was dark and humid; my mother lay like a log on the reed mat, half-dazed after four hours of hard labour. The little clothing she wore was ragged and soaked with sweat. Birth is such a sharp shock even for me, the one who has been borne by women of different creeds.

'You should get rid of this thing, Nokwakha!'

'What?' my mother gushed forward in astonishment.

'Get rid of this thing this moment!' the midwife screeched.

My mother sat upright, steaming with wild fury; a baffled look was written across her face as she stared with contempt at the old wrinkled woman.

'This is a bad omen; you've given birth to an albino. This is the devil incarnate; get rid of this thing at once,' she screamed.

'This is my child!' My mother snatched me from the midwife's arms.

'We should drown this ghost of a child in the nearest river,' the midwife whispered the words with much tenderness this time around. 'The ancestors have warned me countless times to look out for an albino child who would be born in the first moon of spring,' she trembled with fear.

'This girl, I was told, would bring confusion that would lead to the demise of our tribe; she would bring nothing but illusion and we will all jump willingly down the mighty high cliffs of Zambezi to our deaths. The ancestors said she would make false promises to the whole tribe about receiving a gift of immortality in the everlasting life,' the wide-eyed old woman narrated.

'But this is my unknowing child.' My mother's maternal instinct was having none of it.

'The departed ones told me that I would recognise her by the mysterious round hairy black birthmark on her left shoulder blade and I should snuff the life out of her on the spot.'

In an instant, my mother flipped me around to see the birthmark; she stared at it like a lost soul and words refused to come out of her mouth. A bolt of lightning outside induced a loud screech from the base of her gut. She cried like a woman who had just lost a child; buckets of rain fell at that moment and dark heavy clouds hovered in the sky.

'We should get rid of this evil child,' the midwife continued in her persuasion.

The mighty roar of the heavens induced fear in the two women and after some time my mother finally relented under the midwife's spell and agreed to get rid of the unwanted child and so they plotted a plan of action moving forward.

The midwife grabbed the little child by the right ankle and neatly wrapped my whole body with an old cloth and they left for the mighty Umfolozi River. They crawled in the thick tall grass to shy away from any prying eyes. The rain came pouring down and gallons of water quickly filled the river. The wrinkled woman didn't think twice about throwing me down the flowing river to my death; they returned home and never looked back.

A portal to the land of spirits momentarily opened up; a radiant luminous colourless light of emptiness spoke of blissful serenity and deep peace, calling me to the land of origins. I could hear the children of the star giggling and playing the games we used to play and for a moment I wished I was among them. The access to the spirit world opened very briefly; however, my attachment to the almighty purpose made me resist the call to be completely spirit. The two women didn't know that I was under the direct protection of the all-knowing Qamata with a calling to serve. They didn't know that I had one foot trusted in the land of the holy ones and the other in this contemptuous life suspended between birth and death. I was rescued by a middle-aged woman, who found me on the banks of the flowing river. She had been fasting and praying for rain for nine days near the Mpelazwe waterfall. She had only asked for rain to nourish her dying crops but got far more than that. She took me to her home and tried to resuscitate me. She fed me different concoctions to bring me back to this world of form; I remained unconscious. I kept hearing the voices of angels; sons and daughters of the supreme; friendly faces of those I spent most of my time with. I could hear them laughing and making sounds so pure they made my heart melt and almost convinced me to answer their call; they were so near yet so far. I knew I had an earthly mission to serve; a call to honour the commands of the high one.

The two women thought that death was final; they didn't

know that it was merely a figment of their imagination. There is no end for a spirit. The soul is in a state of becoming; a continuous state of learning and development. It does not need the physical body to survive. It continues to exist outside the physical actuality and even outside the apparent life; experience has served this divine truth many times and I accept. When one experiences the 'perceived death', only to be followed by the reality of another existence, a weird sense of divine comedy sets in; realising that the end was only the beginning.

Chos' chosi ngabali.

Two

My present existence in the world of form is probably the most challenging one and I've lived many lifetimes to know that. It is not the bitter and unrelenting changing fixations that this world throws at regular intervals but the multidimensional possibilities in the world of origins that test my purity. There is no one spirit world existing in one dimension like there is no one planet in the universe; one has to die many times before reaching my present plane of existence. I now find it hard to strike a seamless symphony between the form and the formless. The bridge between the two existences needs to be clear of all rubble to truly serve the divine purpose and to be able to pass messages from beyond.

As a little girl growing up, I always felt I was something more than a physical being imprisoned within flesh and bone. There was always a 'me' more pronounced outside the corporeal image; a 'me' that possessed all the enchantment of the spirit. I spent a lot of time gazing lustfully at all the open spaces, admiring all things holy; I listened to the whispering silence for the peace of God. The world of form never really made sense; there were questions more than answers. I was lost in the divine game. The world around me seemed to be talking or at least trying to convey a message; however,

I wasn't ready to comprehend it. The guises of the world of form clouded the truth in the meaning. I was listening and hearing but could not deduce the language locked in symbols. I could feel a pull of vibration begging for my absolute attention. The elders noticed my eyes appeared forever absent-minded.

My aunt, Nontsebenzo calls me Thonqo, 'the stupid one'. She sometimes snaps her fingers at the fall of my face to bring me back to the apparent reality.

'Wathwetyulwa lo mntana kodwa, sisi,' she told my mother. 'This is really a ghost of a child that you have brought into our home, my loving sister,' shaking her head in bewilderment.

My adopted mother is a sangoma, a healer of Bantu; she loves me more than life itself. She calls me by many names, her favourite being Nkwenkwezi; a star of the heavens. As a small child I noticed I was treated differently; I saw it in the eyes of the grown-ups. Their eyes mirrored the most puzzling of emotions and something told me that my mother was overcompensating with her great kindness; strange and fantastic is the stigma a child with albinism experiences. I grew up with song, love and dance and our homestead was and still is forever full with seekers.

My mother is overprotective. She wouldn't let me out of her sight until recently, while girls my age have been playing games in all corners of our village for as long as I can remember. I never understood the height of her panic the moment I drifted out of her sight to play with the other kids.

'Nwelezelanga … Nwelezelanga!' she would shout at the top of her voice with deep anxiety.

'What do I say to you all the time, huh?' A condescending expression would accompany the spirited force of her words.

'You must play in the homestead and not wander about this whole village,' she would reprimand.

It is only now that I understand her over-protectiveness;

there is a belief across the breadth and plains of the land that children with albinism have special powers and our body parts are believed to possess powerful omens by the witches of dark magic. Most of us are hunted down for sacrifices because of the suppositious belief that immortality will be gained in the everlasting life.

It is true that I am addressed by the unseen. Most of my spiritual companions 'visit' every now and then and share holy privileges that I cannot easily access in my present plane of existence. Sometimes we communicate telepathically. We don't use words as such but rather images and symbols that are capable of supporting more expansive meaning and sense. We don't take life too seriously; creative play is very much part of conscious creation. My mother has caught me countless times while addressing these personalities without physical body and initially dismissed them as imaginary friends I've created.

'Uyawathetha nothikoloshe, Nwelezelanga!' She would scoff at me about talking to these invisible beings.

She initially thought I had a curious over-imagination and regarded my engagements with these shades of nothing as harmless and childish but had a change of heart as time progressed. I guess it also helps that she is connected with the world of the spirits through her ancestors; talking with formless beings isn't really taboo to her.

I watch the story of life unfold in the clouds while herding cattle; it is a story of my existence. The purpose of any given lifetime is available but only beneath the surface. One has to scratch and search consciously for the absolute truth to be revealed. I 'travel' to many other levels of existence in search of the evasive truth; it is a crazy existence indeed.

The herdboys poke fun at me every moment they succumb to boredom; it doesn't help that I'm the only shepherd among the boys. They call me names; their favourite is Nongayindoda, the one who resembles a man, because of my chosen chore. I suppose it doesn't help that I don't play with girls my age in the village. I choose to be with the boys because they don't provoke me all the time. The boys are more preoccupied with making life forms out of clay, hunting rabbits, catching insects and stick-fighting; some of the many fascinations they busy themselves with while determining the alpha male ranking order. I'm the least of their worries most of the time. I've had to fight to earn respect though. Stick-fighting is the only respectable way the boys know to separate the machos from the weaklings. It is a wonder to some of the boys that I'm not swollen with pride because of my clean sweep in the art of stick-fighting. I've fallen and humiliated many boys and sent them packing to obscurity. They don't know that I've lived a series of male lives in my past reincarnations and as a result there is a hidden male in my psychical memory and inner self that helps me to not over-identify with my present sex. Most girls my age amplify their female characteristics. My femininity acts as a mellowing feature to the past strong aggressive tendencies that are genetically coded and imbedded in the deeper inner self.

My last victim was a boy called Dambuza. He wasn't full of glory at my past victories. He continuously mocked the shameful lads that succumbed to my whipping.

'I'll never be beaten by a girl, even in my sleep,' he teased their wounded egos. 'I'll beat the golden-haired Nongayindoda with one arm behind my back.'

It was no secret that the fat Dambuza wanted to fight and was rather troubled by how skilfully I managed to stay out of the battle. I wasn't really particular in proving a point. I was more interested with the peculiar world of wonder afforded by the wilderness. I was fascinated by anthills; as the cattle grazed, I would busy myself with watching the ants live their lives. Something within me resonated with the deep and profound world they created. I couldn't help feeling that they were the lost royal rulers of the ancient world. Dambuza thought otherwise. He took a sharp rock and destroyed the royal palace of the ants with the intention of provoking me. He succeeded.

'What are you doing you sweaty fat pig?' Outrage lights up my eyes.

He smiled mischievously and threw two sticks at the bottom of my feet. The smile quickly transformed into a fierce and intense grimace, with his piercing eyes hungry for war. I was furious at the senseless act wielded upon the royal ants. I threw caution to the battlefield. Dambuza was all over me like a possessed demon, swinging his sticks with lightning speed. My defences had to be firm to stave off the onslaught. Once, he caught me off guard and flogged my ribs. I remained calm; this wasn't only my fight, in my mind I was fighting for a higher cause defending the underdog. The other boys gasped in amazement as the intense battle unfolded in front of their eyes under the all-watching heavens. I remained on the defensive as Dambuza was in a hurry to swing victory his way. He tried to hit me on my left ankle but I blocked him and delivered a blow to his ribs. He smiled at the fact that I managed to outmanoeuvre him this once. The battle was balanced. Pride was at stake and time stood still. We both had good defensive abilities. The other boys cheered, urging one of us to deliver the killer blow. Dambuza shuffled back, forth and sideways impressing the crowd with his footwork and a group of his close allies whistled in acknowledgement of his flair. He managed to break my defence once again and hit me on the left knee. He flashed a crooked smile and came forward with much more zeal to end the battle once and for all. He circled me, looking for another opening with surety in his eyes. He pounced on me in a rapid action, swinging the sticks in a concerted assault but I stood my ground and defended with all my might. He retreated to catch his breath. Heat overwhelmed his hippopotamus frame and sweat dripped from his forehead, blurring his eyesight; for a moment he dropped all concentration and attended to the salty itch in his eyes. I stepped forward and delivered a blow to his right ankle. I delivered another one to the left and he came crashing down and bellowed a stinging cry like a little child. The other boys were initially surprised that the mighty Dambuza had fallen but a chorus of laughter cascaded thereafter.

All hail the underdog; the triumph is your crown. Blessed are the meek and the egoless, for they inherit the divine power.

Amen.

Three

In the course of my multiple existences I've learnt to trust more what can't be seen. I am wiser and far more in tune in the dream state. I've come to realise that the dreamworld is more concrete than the world of form and one cannot trust the physical senses to provide a true and comprehensive sense of reality. The dream state allows me the freedom to move through the thin veils of the different worlds. I visit the lands where immortals reside and bathe in their wisdom. The dream-self carries the memories of past existence and opens the path to the infinite. I 'travel' to many other levels of existence in order to fulfil my other duties. In essence, I am a messenger. I'm the voice who speaks without a tongue of my own.

All the knowing is within reach but I cannot claim all the know-how in unlocking the astounding supremacy of the wise sage within; Nomkhubulwana acts as my guide to unravel the deeper truths. She shares holy privileges and experiences in this world of the walking dead. She once took me up the notorious mountain gorge of Mount Zibonele. The ravine is known to have swallowed many men, and even warriors, of the surrounding villages. Many have gone up in an attempt to conquer the mountain and dig for its everlasting secrets but have fallen short of their quest and never came back. No efforts were ever made to rescue those who were stupid enough or brave enough to venture into the belly of this beast. Everyone in the vast land knows that they mission in this no-go zone at their own peril.

The misty mount hummed a troubled tune the day the old wise woman of the tribe took me up for a life-changing experience. The tranquil melody of birds was non-existent as we undertook our great trek up the mountain cliffs. The sound of the crashing water from the nearby Mpelazwe waterfall overpowered the echoes of the uneasy day. The dense forest at the face of the mountain told stories of many tongues; stories never told to ordinary men. Nomkhubulwana won me over with her great calmness and so fear never took refuge in my heart. She exuded a demeanour of the goddess mother as if the whole world was her creation. I saw exotic animals and it seemed that the higher we went up the mountain the more unearthly the animal kingdom became. A snake with two heads looked at us curiously from a tree above and was awestruck by the confidence in our stride. An antelope with three endearing eyes blew kisses in exhibition of its great kindness and purity. It was as if I was deep in the land of fairies. Snails with shells that glowed all the colours of the rainbow flew by clumsily; they kept bumping themselves on the trunks of the tall trees as if they were deprived of vision. It was a fantastic sight of great proportion indeed. Nomkhubulwana remained mum throughout the journey; we spoke a language devoid of speech. We shared the holy experience, devoured it and digested every meaning.

When we finally reached the summit, we were greeted by a big blue lake that stretched as far as the eye could see and seemed to kiss the horizon at its furthest point. The lake was calm but full of mysticism; knowledge deep in all ages seemed to be lying deep in its depths. Nomkhubulwana led the way and sat on the edge of the gigantic cliff overlooking the faraway lands and dangled her feet. I followed suit and was awestruck by the beauty surrounding us. A few white butterflies danced above the lake, exhibiting all things holy. The shattering beauty manifested all heavenly glory. I found myself breathing heavily as the magnificence of it all surged through every vein in my body. I was spellbound. Nomkhubulwana looked at me and whispered in the tenderest voice that made my heart melt.

'You are different to others,' she said in her angelic voice.

'Yours is a special journey, a messenger of great truths from beyond,' she continued while staring at the vast blue lake.

'My time is running out; my mission is nearing its ultimate purpose but the work undone is still great. There is a sense of elation as I feel "death" knocking at my door; it is coming to announce a completion of a purpose. I have always been aware of my inevitable physical demise and I always saw it as an opportunity to learn from my immediate past life. I always found my "deaths" highly enlightening. There is a pronounced sense of modesty and yet a great sense of ecstasy knowing that true freedom is nearing; it is a process of becoming.'

She turned and looked me straight in the eyes and pierced my soul. My very being was arrested by the overwhelming emotions in her heart. I was showered with the fountain of wisdom deep in the reservoirs of her being.

'The hour is growing late, the world and its perception of form is on its last legs. The source begs us to listen; humanity has to take a leap of faith. The natural kingdom groans in pangs for God's sons and daughters to take a conscious evolutionary leap. The walking dead cannot anymore assume the perishable norms and walk on the thorny plains like there's nothing astounding unfolding. We, the ones who see, the children of the star, are here to reveal the great truth staring humanity in the face but that seems forever blind to its brightness.'

For a moment the self and the other were one in every fibre.

I listened with the ears of my soul and let it all sink in. She continued to dish out pearls of wisdom.

'Human beings do not know that they are sons and daughters of gods so they themselves are gods. They live under the illusion that they are lesser than what they truly are. They don't know that the kingdom awaits them to sit at the throne and unlock all the knowledge within and all the untold stories deep in all ages. Ours is to release the wise sage in all the walking dead.' A single glistening tear fell down her left cheek.

Nomkhubulwana suddenly knelt and prayed in three languages. It wasn't a structured language of ordinary words, she was in communion using the language of old as if addressing the very beginning of time; at times she hissed guttural and grunting sounds full of emotions with profound spectacle. She was reaching out to the god of gods, deep in the ten gates of eternity. She was deep in the pious act when I noticed her levitate inches from the ground. A white unicorn with an elegant flowing mane and tail ran magically in impressive grandeur across the lake to the furthest point and disappeared into the blue horizon. Rain fell at that moment; it drizzled and blessed the day with awe and rejuvenation, and then a rainbow so magnificent hovered above the majestic lake. I was lost in a dream. The messages opened every valve of emotion in my heart. These are messages from beyond that I now carry.

Be humble to the supreme; there's power in complete surrender. Everything else is secondary. You are connected to the source.

Four

BEING BORN INTO THIS world of mortals was a trauma I never fully recovered from. Though it was my living wish to come into this land of the walking dead, nothing prepares us, the children of the star, for the abrupt separation from the warm world of dreams. My earliest memory was the overwhelming love my mother showered me with. I was the apple of her eye, a miracle baby who cheated death, a baby who wanted to live despite the curtains of forever-night closing in on her. Mama always tells me that I'm a blessed child; a child who came with rain when there was drought in the village.

The cock crows in the wee hours of the morning; Mama is already up grinding a dry tobacco leaf for her snuff. The smell of the burning everlasting plant, impepho, circulates in the hut.

'Good morning my child,' Mama greets.

'Morning Ma,' I woozily reply.

'Wake up my child, an early bird catches the freshest worm,' she says.

'Yes, Mama,' I reply.

In an instant, I wake up, fold my blankets and hang them on the thread attached to the left side of the circling interior wall. I roll up my reed mat and place it at the north end of the room.

'Prepare porridge quickly Nkwenkwezi, we need to go to the maize fields and remove the nuisance weeds as the break of day greets. I have a feeling that it's going to be a scorching day and we don't want to be weathered by the unmerciful sun, especially you my child,' she instructs.

I make my way to the hut where meals are prepared to fetch a bucket to collect water from the nearby stream. I love the tranquillity of the early hours of the morning. The breeze caresses while the three-quarter moon is completing its lap. The morning dew on the path sobers me to a more awake state. The calmness of the day soothes the spirit. My mind moves to all seven corners of time without really settling on one thought. I'm lost in the seven winds. A brass band of frogs bellows melodramatically as I approach the stream while the crickets add their musical prowess to the early morning orchestra. The moon and the stars reflect magically in the water as if heaven has visited our land. I wash my face in the flowing water and take a sip. I collect the water with the bucket and balance it on top of my head on my way back to the homestead. The sound of a stone grinding the dry tobacco leaf still echoes in the big hut when I arrive back home; one can be sure that the process of making her snuff in the early hours of the morning is meditative for Mama. I take the axe from the shed and make myself useful by splitting the logs to appropriate chunks for the fire.

'I'll need to get thinner wood from the forest later today.' The thought flashes through my mind.

I wash one of the three-legged cast-iron pots and prepare the fire to boil water for the porridge.

'Nkwenkwezi?' Mama calls from the big hut.

She is the only one who calls me Nkwenkwezi; I know that she is in a good mood when she does so.

'Yes, Mama.'

'Pick up some nice lemons for me; you know that I like my porridge sour.'

'Yes, Mama.'

I dash to the garden in front of the semicircle of huts to pick the lemons. I also pick ripe peaches for us to eat while we are working in the maize fields. I serve the porridge to Mama moments later.

'Go wake up your Aunt Nontsebenzo and your sister, they must eat; we need to get going soon.'

'Okay Mama.'

The birds sing a beautiful melody in their waking hour as the light begins to lift the veil for the start of a new day. Aunt Nontsebenzo and my sister Zimasa join us in the big hut. I quickly dish up and serve them porridge.

'Oh, I had an awful dream, my sister,' Aunt Nontsebenzo begins to tell the nocturnal tale while she stirs her porridge.

'What was the dream about, my little sister?' Mama asks inquisitively.

'Light another impepho and tell me more about it,' Mama instructs Aunt Nontsebenzo.

She always insists that impepho is lit when we relay our dreams early in the morning. She says that the ancestors were so kind to visit us at nightfall to pass on holy privileges and we should return the favour and invite them back when telling our nocturnal ventures.

'I dreamt a wildcat came to our home at night and attacked the chickens as they slept in the shed. The unusual thing was that it wasn't eating the spoils but kept unleashing death until all the chickens lay dead on the floor,' Aunt Nontsebenzo narrates with perplexed emotions on her face.

'What could this dream possibly mean, sisi?' she asks Mama in distress.

Mama ponders the truth in the meaning. She takes the burning impepho and inhales the smoke and whispers to her ancestors, calling them by name to untangle the riddle presented to her. She looks at Aunt Nontsebenzo and shares her divination.

'The ultimate meaning will probably be revealed in time; the departed ones work in unknown ways; sometimes they are not in a rush to reveal the deeper truth. You must burn impepho before you sleep this evening and ask the all-seeing of old to reveal the full meaning of this dream,' Mama tells Aunty.

We sit in silence for a moment; the sound of the spoons touching the plates is thick in the air.

'Let's go now, the lord of day has protruded the horizon. We need to start working to keep up with earth's heartbeat,' says Mama as she stands to her feet.

'Get the hoe from the shed, Nwelezelanga. Zimasa, wash the dishes quickly and join us at the maize fields when you are finished,' instructs Mama to my sister and me.

Many nearby families make their way to the maize fields as the sun rises to do the same job of hoeing and plucking the weeds that surround the crop. It's a necessary task for the maize to blossom without any inhibitions. The work is also contemplative in a way and connects family units deeper. We work in unison with the same goal of an envisioned good harvest. There's little talking but much is being communicated in a language free of speech. The hoe does the talking and doing in turning the earth and plucking the weeds. Jokes do fly around at times; that's one of the tricks I observe Mama use to make us not think too much about the hard labour at hand as strength ebbs and tiredness takes its place.

The sun rises and dominates the day. We work in rhythmic unison, focusing on the work at hand. The exertion takes its toll and beads of sweat fall off the faces of the women at work. We continue hoeing without any conversation connecting us. It seems that everyone has visited a world deep in the forest of their subconscious mind. The sun begins to make me uncomfortable as I start to scratch. My straw hat is no match for the domineering sun. I take a breather, putting the wood handle of the hoe under my armpit and leaning on it while it's planted on the soil. Mama looks at me for a second then continues with her work. Aunt Nontsebenzo and Zimasa seem tireless and full of zest even after the great effort to date.

'Go to the shade now, Nwelezelanga, you know that the sun is unmerciful to you,' Mama instructs with kindness.

'But Mama! Nwelezelanga is up to her old tricks again. There's nothing wrong with her, she is just lazy!' Zimasa interjects and cries foul.

'You know that your sister cannot take the harsh gaze of the sun for long; it blinds her and makes her itch as her skin is very sensitive,' Mama says, coming to my aid.

'She is just too lazy to work, that's all, and you swallow her excuses,' Zimasa wails at Mama with a defeated voice.

'Zimasa, let's not go back and forth with this; this is not a discussion,' Mama responds in a punitive tone.

'Go and rest princess!' Zimasa says to me condescendingly.

I don't respond. I silently make my way to the big yellowwood tree in the middle of the maize fields. I fall on the ground in utter exhaustion. The itch begins to fade as the cool breeze soothes my skin. I close my eyes to suppress the burning sensation and sleep calls in an infectious hum that seduces me to its temple.

I find myself surfing the twilight zone deep under the ocean floor, the inexplicable land of paramount earth. There are festivities and jubilations as the chosen ones prepare to take a journey to the land of mortals. The high spirits paint the scene with holy messages. All preparations are done to acclimatise those who are taking the momentous journey of being born. There are speeches made by the old wise ones about the journey ahead and much is being said in silence that speaks volumes. The rituals are meant to impress the very souls of the spirits taking the journey to the land of the walking dead so as not to forget their divine selves and also prepare them to swim without self-doubt in the sea of ignorance. A voice from the all-knowing Qamata ricochets in all corners of the known and unknown world.

'The passage you are about to embark on is not an easy one. Many see this journey as a fall from grace; however, you have the task to untangle the mysteries of existence and share your wisdom with fellow men as part of your development to higher planes,' the booming voice echoes.

'The greater part of this journey is to remain true to what you truly are; sons and daughters of the supreme.' There's much emphasis behind the words.

'Always remember that you are spiritual beings suspended in momentary physical existence; ignorance to your divine self will be your greatest sin.' The all-knowing Qamata plants the message deep in their souls.

A flashing blinding light accompanied by a thunderous clamour follows as the spirits take the earth-shattering passage through the seas to the world of form. I don't know how long I was among the all-seeing of old before I hear Mama calling my name.

'Nwelezelanga!'

'Nwelezelanga!' Mama calls out a second time.

'Why are you sleeping in the maize field, huh?' Obvious anger boils her temper.

'You know it's a bad omen sleeping during the day, let alone in the maize field.' She gives me a patronising look accompanied by the spirited force of the words.

In an instant I sit up straight, feeling mortified.

'Bring that jug of amarhewu; we are thirsty and dying of heat.'

I oblige as instructed. I also take the peaches that I picked earlier in an attempt to be on Mama's good side. Everybody takes a break and sits down, munching the peaches and quenching their thirst. The break breeds light-heartedness as everyone momentarily forgets about the hard labour.

Mama begins to tell a story as is the ritual when everyone is feeling tired.

'There was a maiden called Maqalazive who was the gossip-mongering queen of the village; she knew everything that happened in the vast land,' Mama tells the tale of yore.

'Anyone who wanted to know what was happening in the village would invite her for a cup of tea, knowing that she wouldn't be able to hold back on the latest gossip and would jump at the chance to run her mouth off about the dealings of other people.' Mama gets us eating out of the palm of her hands with each word.

'The gossip queen wasn't too particular with facts but was obsessed with the attention she was getting as the conveyor of the bush telegraph. On one occasion she visited her new neighbour for the first time and after the formal exchange of pleasantries, without any invitation, she let loose on the latest gossip. She told the new neighbour about a woman who killed her husband because she loved the older brother of her husband,' Mama narrates with dramatic exhibition.

'She didn't realise that the lies she was peddling were to the sister of the widow.' Mama's face lights up.

'The neighbour asked her meticulously about the details of her narration and was disgusted and angry at the fabrications that came from the wild motormouth. She quietly took a whip that was hanging behind the door and began beating the gossip queen without telling her the reason for the royal beating. The woman ran outside crying foul and the new neighbour was in hot pursuit so as to continue whipping her. Maqalazive didn't know why she was beaten but later found out via the village gossip mill.' Mama leads a chorus of laughter.

Everyone joins in and the moment is filled with nonchalance. The sun dances and smiles, seemingly enjoying the task of lighting and warming up the day. Swallows fly effortlessly with flare and easy flamboyance in the clear sky. Villagers in the nearby homesteads work tirelessly in their maize fields.

'Let's pluck out the weeds in three more rows and then we can call it a day; we'll continue with the rest of the work tomorrow morning.' Mama rings the bell to go back to work.

We all pick our hoes up off the ground and get back to work for the last stretch of the day.

'Inyoka!' Zimasa exclaims upon seeing a snake.

'Yoh, yoh, yoh!' Aunt Nontsebenzo cries out and leaps away from the slithering reptile.

'Where is it?'Mama asks Zimasa.

'There it is!' Zimasa points at the snake.

'Where?' Mama asks again with her eyes fixed on the area Zimasa is pointing to.

'There, by that dry patch. Look, look, it's moving!' Zimasa points at the moving snake.

Mama sees the snake and approaches it slowly with the stealth of a seasoned predator. She takes two more steps towards it with her hoe held high above her right shoulder and with a rapid movement smashes the snake in the middle of its spine with the back of the hoe. The snake twists and turns in agony and Mama hits its head twice.

'Got it,' whispers Mama under her breath.

The snake is dead but the tail twitches sporadically. Mama kneels and takes out the snuff from her pouch. She sprinkles some on the head of the snake and then sniffs it into both her nostrils; her eyes water. She says to the 'dead' snake, 'By the power vested in me to slay you; I shall also be slayed by the more powerful.'

She thanks her ancestors, calling generations and generations of those of yore by name in a deeply respectful act.

'Come see Nontsebenzo; a dead snake cannot bite,' Mama makes fun of Aunt Nontsebenzo.

'Yhu, sisi, you know me and snakes are not friends at all,' says Aunt Nontsebenzo with fear glistening in her popping eyes.

'Oh come on, it's dead!' says Mama with spirited force in her voice.

Aunt Nontsebenzo cautiously walks closer to the snake with her eyes full of distress.

'It's dead, Aunty,' Zimasa says, putting Aunt Nontsebenzo at ease.

'Yoh, it's big!' shouts Aunt Nontsebezo upon seeing the snake close up.

'It's not that big, you coward,' Mama shoots back.

Mama picks up the dead snake with a stick and inspects the breed with her trained eye.

'I'll use it for my medicine,' she says with a delighted smile.

'A correct dose of poison mixed with other herbs can be a healing medicine,' she says wisely.

'Let's finish for the day, my children. Nwelezelanga, carry my hoe and take that jug with you, Zimasa,' Mama instructs.

Mama leads the way, carrying the dead snake with the stick. The work for the day is complete. Mama says we work in order to grow and keep up with the earth's heartbeat. She says that the earth is for our sustenance. We don't own it, we are of the earth. The red soil of the hills and valleys of the land communicates with us about pertinent matters of the heart. She says in working with the soil our spirits are purified.

Tread softly on the ageless soil; listen with the soles of your bare feet. Camagu!

Five

I CHOSE THIS LIFE with all its pitfalls because I was becoming too blasé in the world of the spirits; I was too cushioned. I no longer paid much attention to the true experience the land of the living dead provided. I was slowly forgetting the power of suffering, and while suffering isn't necessary for redemption, it is true that suffering makes us grow. When one realises that the 'lowest point' is actually the 'highest point'; acknowledging that in the midst of the 'unfavourable situation' lies the deepest truth, magic happens.

We, the children of the star, have crossed so many rivers, sailed in the wayward high winds of the great oceans, have been born in the obscurest dwellings and died so many 'deaths' in order to be born again. We are the willing explorers into adversities and we transmute the adversities into magnificence. We seek the light and the light introduces us to darkness so that we shed the light with more meaning. We collide with experiences not willing to be brought into existence and they ask us to incubate them before their earth-shattering birth. We are the charmed sacrifice because we said, 'Yes, savuma', we said 'yes' to the calling and enlightenment wholeheartedly. We wander down the road less travelled to feel more and contribute more. We chose the road and the road chose us. Our hearts yearn for the unchartered terrains. We plunge into notorious riddles in order to untangle the hidden wisdom. Pain knows our hearts and we know pain as the necessary friend in growth. Wavering intensity of emotions fills our hearts to give us zest to move forward with indomitable passion. We are the alchemists, turning suffering into joy; a true magnificent manifestation of the philosopher's stone. We embrace the fullness of life and have all the scars to prove it. This is the life that chose us. We have a purpose to serve and our feelings act as a compass to shed more light. In following our purpose, we realise that we are creating paths in virgin territories that can also be used by others.

'Nwelezelanga!' Mama calls from outside.

'Maaaaa,' I reply from the big hut.

'Bring me a small knife, my child,' she asks.

I find Mama sitting in a patch of grass near the kraal. I pass the knife to her and she cuts the snake down its side, starting at the corner of its mouth, down to the tip of its tail. She opens it up, exposing all the insides. She cuts out all the inside fat and puts it in the jar adjacent to her. She then cuts out the bile and puts it in a separate jar. A whole mouse is still lodged in the intestines of the snake. Mama takes it out and puts it in another jar.

'We are not going to throw away the mouse; it has some of the medicine we need as its body is riddled with poison.'

Mama takes the snake and hangs it on a pole near the entrance of the kraal in order for it to dry out to use to make medicine.

'It will be good medicine for protection and once I mix it with other herbs my enemies won't come near me,' says Mama with a childish gloat.

The cows moo in the kraal.

'Take the cows to the grazing field, Nwelezelanga, they are hungry,' Mama tells me softly.

'Are the chickens fed? Where's Zimasa?' she asks.

'I don't know Ma, I think Zimasa went to the nearby stream to wash clothes,' I reply.

'Please feed the chickens then, my child, before you let the cows out.'

'Okay, Mama.'

I oblige and dash to the big hut to get some maize to feed the chickens.

'Kuuuuk, kuuuuk, kukukukukuk!' I call out to the chickens.

They come running from the different corners of the homestead, flapping their wings and jostling to fill their stomachs with the corn I've scattered on the ground in front of the semicircle of huts. They eat in a frenzy as if it's their last meal in this life.

I let the cattle out of the kraal on our way to the grazing field near the hills overlooking the Vezinyawo forest. I love the docile beasts, they are humble and calm with eyes revealing their deepest emotions. They bring ease to my spirit as if I have been touched by the hand of the old wise one. We understand each other and communicate in a language we both know. They teach me about the deeper essence and share holy privileges. They have taught me that patience is the friend of the wise. Most herdboys seem to be blind to their hidden wisdom though; some boys are forever beating the cattle, screaming instructions, thinking that they are lazy and stupid.

I marvel at the wilderness and all things holy as the cattle graze; the natural kingdom is a great teacher in many ways. I'm fascinated by the different birds and their arch of connection which makes them tranquil in flight and telepathic in communication. I watch the swallows fly with fine flamboyance and flaunt the divine essence with grace, finesse and deep passion. My spirit lets go and flies to the different corners of the soul sphere. I watch the clouds tell prophesies in abstract symbols full of meaning and sense. It's as if I've been cast over by a spell as the morphing clouds hold my absolute attention seeking to reveal messages from beyond. It is a struggle to decode some of the messages locked in symbols. The forest is calm yet vibrant in telling stories never told; stories that speak directly to the matters of the heart. The tall trees whistle gentle melodies of the different ages in the book of life. The mood of the Vezinyawo forest invokes the essence. The feeling seduces my very being and I somehow wish I could be lost in its embrace forever. The trees pass messages that are urgent and of utmost importance while being rooted in their wisdom and humility. I see a flashing shadow image of one of the children of the star coming to existence and disappearing into thin air. I wonder if I'm hallucinating as a result of missing them too much. A moment later, I see some ghost images of those I recognise from the playground of eternity behind the fat trunk of a baobab tree. I run towards the tree to expose them from their hiding place. They vanish as I approach them and I hear their chorus of chuckles merrily swept away by the impartial winds. The scents from the different flowers flavour the moment with pure innocence. I chase the butterflies up and down the hills but it seems that they are purposefully leading me to discoveries. I tumble down the hill like a log into a shrub of lilies and then a bold voice comes from the lilac tree not too far away.

'There is nothing to matter at all; it's all spiritual. Do not gravitate the essence to a dense state thereby making things matter. It's all spiritual in essence. Even the rock you are sitting on is no matter, it is energy; it is formless in its truest essence. It's all spiritual; rise and realise that there is nothing to matter.' The flowering shrub with fragrant violet flowers speaks profoundly.

I am awestruck by the validity of the moment. I am free to experience the celestial because my heart of hearts yearns to be swept away by feelings never experienced in the deeper corridors of the soul sphere. I delight in the majestic pleasures of the higher order. A stern voice from the flowering shrub echoes once again.

'Only by going to the deepest depths of self to feel and perceive the true nature of your being can you glimpse the nature of all that is.'

I'm reminded of my past reincarnation as a baobab tree; I delighted in the simple pleasures, indulging in relaxation for more than a century, yet creating the forest in which I grew. I was bare and open, willing to share for the better. I honoured the divine and connected with the deeper essence which made possible the fulfilling of the true spiritual force within.

The sun lowers in the distant horizon and prepares to set. The changing winds blanket the plains with chilly bites and messages from the faraway gods. I make my way down the hill to round up the cattle; some of them have disappeared in the lush forest while others still graze at the foot of the hill. We follow the setting sun on our way back to the homestead. The other herdboys also make their way back home with their herds of cattle. The sun sets behind the Mojaji mountain but the golden glow of its rays paints the horizon with magical undertones. A column of smoke from the different homesteads reaches up for the sky as the village women prepare supper on outside fires. I arrive home as the dark veil of night begins to cover the land. I put the cattle in the kraal and close the entrance. My stomach growls in anticipation of the evening meal. I make my way to the big hut.

'Did you manage to bring back the whole herd, my child?' Mama asks.

'Yes, Mama,' I reply in a low weary tone.

'You look tired my child; take your plate of food from the table before these naughty cats steal your meat.' Mama offers me supper.

'What's the occasion? Why was a chicken slaughtered?' I enquire curiously.

'I don't need a reason to slaughter a chicken. I can do so

whenever I want,' Mama replies defensively.

'Don't you want the meat, Nwelezelanga?' Aunt Nontsebenzo butts in.

'I'm just asking, Aunty; you know Mama hardly slaughters anything without a ceremonial reason,' I emphasise my point.

'And she loves her precious domestic fowls more than us,' Zimasa chips in.

'You girls want to eat up all my livestock,' Mama lashes out jokingly.

'Ningamazim!'

Everyone dissolves into laughter. A jovial mood circulates the big hut before Aunt Nontsebenzo cuts the atmosphere with breaking news.

'Have you heard the rumours going around about Nwelezelanga, sisi?'

'You know that I'm too busy to keep up with the petty gossip of this village, Nontsebenzo.' Mama is dismissive yet interested in what Aunt Nontsebenzo has to say.

'Okay, let me fill you in, sisi. The herdboys say that your precious daughter has been seen talking to shrubs and shades of nothing like a demented lunatic while the cattle graze.' Aunt Nontsebenzo shares the gossip.

'Oh, the people of this village can talk and talk until they are blue in the face, they don't know that this child has rare gifts,' Mama says in my defense.

'What do you mean, sisi?' asks Aunt Nontsebenzo.

'Nwelezelanga is not like other children; she sees things that no other people see,' Mama continues in her persuasion.

'Ay, I don't follow, my sister,' says Aunt Nontsebenzo mystified.

'Nwelezelanga feels and acknowledges the life in everything, even the rock that you think is dead, she can speak to its life form. She is a clairvoyant child capable of telling future histories; she is sensitive to her most inner self, ithongo lalo mntana linzima.'

'Oh Mama, you love this child of yours too much and are willing to find excuses for her demented ways,' Zimasa joins the conversation.

'Hawu, why are you talking about me like I'm not in the room?' I finally exclaim.

'We are not talking to you, we are talking about you. Deal with it!' Zimasa interjects harshly.

'One day it will be one of you who'll talk to shrubs and you will know what I'm talking about,' Mama carries on.

'Never!' Zimasa cries out.

'I know they say that one must never say never but I will say never,' Aunt Nontsebenzo states unequivocally.

'Never is a long time, Nontsebenzo. I'm a sangoma and I see more than an average person and I'm telling you that this is a blessed child. She brought rain when there was drought in the land.'

'Yoh sisi, I rest my case. I see this beloved daughter of yours has cast a spell on you,' says Aunt Nontsebenzo in a defeated voice.

'I understand you my little sister, you don't know what you don't know,' says Mama finally.

There's a recognisable heavy silence in the air. Mama unexpectedly bursts into song in the tenderest voice that makes my insides quiver. She stands up and slowly moves in a rhythmic motion, feeling every note of the melody. She gets lost in the song.

'Where is the drum?' she asks while her eyes remain wide shut.

The drum has always spoken profoundly to me before I could talk and walk. I always felt a release to higher planes the moment I heard the booming sound of the ancient musical instrument of the land. It told the history of our tribe; stories that carry us to this day.

Zimasa joins the song and dance with the drum and a wild savage exhibition ensues. Mama stamps the ground with passion, feeling the booming sound of the drum; her whole upper body shakes as if possessed by alien spirits. She spins and spins like a top as if she could lift off into the night sky. We clap with more zeal to lift her higher and higher to higher planes. She leaps up and then stamps the ground with gusto. The singing and dancing uplifts energies. The essence has taken over and raises the spirits. All matters of the world don't seem to matter. The gravitational force that is dense in matter is overpowered by the supreme force of lightness. We rise in song; the booming sound moves through the veins. The dance exudes the highness and lightness of spirit. Mama's feet are almost not touching the ground; her personality changes like waves of light showing off supreme charisma, grace, humility, love and lightness of being.

I follow the music and it takes me up the sacred mountains and deep into its caves in search of the forbidden knowledge. I follow the mesmerising rhythm in ascension to the clouds, far away where space and time don't matter. I visit unknown worlds in a trance while my very soul is arrested by the sound of the beating drum. I am a willing prisoner to its rhythm. I see all of the nine gods of the nine heavens from the highway of eternity. The almighty Qamata steals my heart and rests it in his almighty kingdom in one spellbinding moment. The activities reach the very peak of elation and Mama starts making grunting sounds, communicating with her ancestors. She thanks them for keeping us safe until this day; she thanks them for the revelations that open our paths moving forward. She asks them to continue looking over us and to guide us on the thorny plains of this contemptuous existence. The drum echoes faintly behind her intuitive prayer; it is medicine for the restless soul.

In essence, the drum is a healer of Bantu. Kaboom!

Six

It is true that the wise elders overstate their kindness towards us most of the time in an effort to lure us away from the fact that most villagers find children with albinism strange. We are treated as freaks, accidents of nature, and are relegated to being outcasts in our land. We get special attention because we do not look like the others. The elders speak nicely to us, something that is rare as there is a belief in our tribe that one should not be praised as one will become big-headed and egotistical and lose track of one's good behaviour. Girls my age resent the attention I get and in return ridicule me, telling me how unnatural I am. Sometimes I wish I could change my life and receive less attention from the adults so that girls my age would not tease me so much.

A knock reverberates from the door as we are drifting to a world of dreams; the knock whispers with rhythm and with a concealed urgent notice.

'Ngubani lowo?' Mama enquires loudly.

'Nomkhubulwana,' the faceless voice responds.

'Haaa?' Mama enquires once again.

'Nomkhubulwana,' the woman repeats her name.

Mama gets up and lights a candle. She makes her way to the door and opens it hesitantly.

'Camagu Makhosi,' Nomkhubulwana greets Mama with some reservation.

'Forgive me for coming at this late hour to your homestead; I have an urgent and important matter that needs your attention, Gogo. I had a vision that I wanted to relay to you that involves your daughter. Can you come outside for a second so that we can discuss the matter in private?' she humbly asks.

Mama goes outside to listen to what Nomkhubulwana has to say. I can hardly hear their whispers. The murmurs carry on for a while; Mama comes back into the hut after some time and calls my name.

'Nwelezelanga.' Her voice cuts the still of the night.

'Nomkhubulwana has come for you, my child. There's an important journey you have to take with her. Dress warmly, dear child; she is waiting for you outside at the entrance of the kraal,' Mama says with a heavy solemn voice.

In the forest of my subconscious, something tells me that this is a momentous occasion. I make my way out into the night sky. The full moon glows with mystical suggestions and echoes songs of love while the dancing stars sparkle and rejoice in a divine spectacle. They both light the frowning earth with magical undertones. I find Nomkhubulwana sitting next to the entrance of the kraal.

'Please sit down, oh child of light,' she says in a calm voice. 'You have to come with me to the Mpelazwe waterfall; the great Qamata has a task for us to fulfil.' She states the reason for the nightly visit. 'I have taken this journey many times before. It is a call to honour the wishes of the divine one.'

She says a prayer quietly and it stills the moment. I'm a willing traveller to the unknown. The cattle in the kraal act as witness to this earthly episode.

'We can go now,' she says coolly.

She stands up and follows the Milky Way. The river of

stars leads us to the east. We pass sleeping villages as we move with purpose. The dogs bark at us, suspicious of our mission. I follow behind the ageing sage; the speaker of great truths takes decisive strides deep into the woods. The moon lights the immense land in a shade darker than day. A hooting owl at the fringes of the forest greets us from a tall tree. We take winding pathways that lead us to the Mpelazwe waterfall. We journey up and down the hills, crossing different streams. The wind carries messages from the different ages as the creatures of the night move secretly behind the bushes. The echoes of the falling water from the waterfall tell us that we are not far from our destination. A shooting star breaks in the atmosphere in a never-ending fall; it travels faster and brighter, then disappears as quickly as it came. Nomkhubulwana has not said a single word in this great trek. We zigzag down the rock face; I tail her religiously down the slope. We reach a flat surface at the edge of the waterfall. The sound of the water overpowers the moment; a profound sense of tranquillity arrests my very being.

Nomkhubulwana takes a shiny copper coin from her pouch and says a silent prayer before throwing the coin into the waterfall. She then lights a candle and some dry leaves of the sage plant. She kneels and I follow her, hypnotised by the ceremony. She inhales the smoke from the burning leaves and gestures for me to do the same. The smell unlocks a window and opens several gateways to eternity. A heavy cloud ready to give birth stations itself in front of the moon and diminishes its glow for a moment; it drizzles heavenly showers and blesses the occasion.

'Thank you!'

'Thank you, Siyabulela!' Nomkhubulwana shouts in all humbleness, expressing gratitude.

She takes a few more copper coins from her pouch. She encloses them in the palms of her hands and shakes them steadily, listening attentively to the sound they make. She bursts into prayer with a gifted tongue. She continues to shake the coins and her upper body trembles as if being transported to upper actualities. She throws the coins high in the air and they scatter in different directions on the flat rock surface.

Nomkhubulwana lifts both her hands up with her palms facing the all-knowing heavens. She speaks in tongues, using the language of old. She swallows my very being into her prayer and I serve as a witness and creator of dreams. We receive and plant dreams for the sleeping villages; opening highways to various dimensions. We act as guides to the dreamers as they journey to the forgotten territories of the soul sphere. We fulfil the higher order by translating messages from beyond to more recognisable symbols. We act as vessels in communicating the absolute truth of all eternity. We pray in unison with every valve of emotion open to receive and give.

A 'cloud' of prayer full of holy messages rises and flies away, covering the land and planting wisdom in all living souls. The prayer visits the deepest depths of the soul sphere of the dreamers. The prayer influences the dream-self of the sleeping souls to take a more prominent role; awaking the living form to a more attune divine state by accessing forgotten territories to true divinity. We plant messages from the different worlds in the subconscious, just below the window of awareness; whispering gently the echoes of the dreamers' divine destinies yet to come. The sacred act carries on until the height of the morning hour. Exhaustion creeps in and overwhelms. I don't know how long we travelled the sacred planes of dreams to fulfil the higher order before descending back to the apparent reality of form. Nomkhubulwana once again lights the dry leaves of the sage plant and says another prayer.

She then looks at me and says, 'A dream is an attempt to articulate the deeper experience in a more recognisable form; in essence, dreams are the roaming of the spirits.' She hypnotises me with her wisdom.

'The images within the dream are highly coded with deeper

meaning and are not decipherable to the one who perceives the world of form as authority,' says Nomkhubulwana, absorbed in the moment.

'We are helpful to those who are ready to go beyond just looking; those who actually see the hidden wisdom. We communicate with those who are ready to go beyond just hearing; those who actually listen to the voices of ancients. We assist them in discovering revelations and inspirations.' She unravels my soul's intentions with a penetrating gaze.

'Those who are divorced from the physical focus are in a better position to hear us, aiding them in translating the abstract symbols communicating their soul's intentions,' she says, thereby revealing our purpose.

'There is a state in the corridors of sleep in which telepathic and clairvoyant messages are received by the dreamer; a state where we become gods and reach out to the different dimensions of the soul sphere. The living dead in their ignorance have put absolute focus in the physical reality and negate the indomitable force of the spirit; a spirit more capable than what the five physical senses perceive. Many refuse to acknowledge that the physical actuality is a by-product of a much deeper reality. There are far more wonders to perceive through this inward exploration. Ours is to remind the walking dead of their true self and assist those who are ready to decipher messages beyond their present state,' she says, adding more of the sage plant to the fading one.

We sit for a while in silence listening to the crashing water; my heart overflows with awe. Another shooting star with a long tail appears then vanishes without trace. The moon smiles and flourishes with love divine. We meditate by resting our minds on the breath to clear all mind activities. Finally, we make our way back home in the darkest hour of the morning. The erect posture that defined our physique at the outset of this great trek has dropped as tiredness overwhelms.

Follow your dreams; they have chosen you as much as you have chosen them. Chosi.

Part Two

Seven

LEGENDS AND MYTHS of the tribe say that in the beginning there was an incredible darkness and the darkness was life. The darkness ruled all the corners and highways of the known and unknown world. All the great orators, prophets, sages, diviners and the wise ones of all ages say that the darkness was an expression of the all-knowing one. Different spirits pervaded the darkness throughout its multidimensionality. There were no permanent structures to symbolise the birth of form and physical actuality; space was all there was and space was not empty. Spirits roamed the different dimensions in great silence that spoke volumes and creativity was the basis of existence.

The folktales say that for aeons and aeons there was harmony in the dark world as it grew to realise more of the self; however, harmony is not free of conflict forever and nothing stays the same for all time; the creative force of friction is necessary for growth and expansion to upper planes.

A certain diabolic spirit proclaimed itself as the lord of darkness and called itself Bubi; it pronounced almighty reign over its band of associate spirits and over time conquered lesser spirits and its kingdom grew far and wide. The foul spirit appointed a high priest, Mpundulu, and a high priestess,

Mthakathi, as commanding superiors of the wicked empire. The delusion of the lord of darkness grew to the very peak of crisis and an extreme was reached.

The natural order has a way of protecting itself when imbalances occur and through some unexplainable cosmic gestation a spark of light brightened the world; the spark of light moved from the source and multiplied in different directions and multidimensions.

Everything upon this earth owes its ancestry to this initial spark of light. The light is growing and reaching the furthest frontiers of the known and unknown world. The soul is that spark of light that continues to manifest itself in different forms. The wise ones say that the Bantu are the descendants of that spark of light that manifested in order to bring balance in a world dominated by darkness and the domineering kingdom of Lord Bubi.

The lord of darkness rules the underworld with an iron fist and robs gullible souls of their divinity and true magnificence, while the high priest and high priestess distort the harmonious energies and thrive with parasite tendencies. They all feed upon ignorance and the pain they inflict on unsuspecting ones.

The knowing ones say that the lord of darkness has illusions that he is the ruler of creation itself and imposes himself as the ultimate high. Over an unimaginable period of time Lord Bubi and his band of spirits have tried their utmost to keep the delusion alive and maintain the status quo that began to crumble when the spark of light lit the darkness. The high priest, Mpundulu, and high priestess, Mthakathi, work tirelessly to shield the light and therefore the truth and convince the spirits of light and the walking dead that they are less than what they actually are. They have succeeded in many respects to convert lower vibrational spirits and some of the walking dead to serve the underworld with the promise that they will rise to a more destructive force.

'Darkness shall dominate both night and day once again for all eternity,' are the vows made by the souls of dark magic.

The old wise ones say that the lord of darkness and his band of spirits drink in the fountain of megalomania and perpetuate 'false facts' to their disillusioned masses, and omit the actual fact that darkness only thrives upon darkness and actually finds light indigestible.

The high priest and high priestess roam the vast land seducing the dream-self of lost souls.

There are many who serve as a representation of darkness across the plains of the rural heartland. The rise of the dark spirits coincides with the rise of the ego. The foul spirits and the walking dead, in their ignorance, separated themselves from the oneness of all that is and bought into the illusion that they are islands of existence.

While the villages sleep, there are those who work overtime secretly performing sadistic rituals to alter the harmonious energy of creation into a nightmare for the passive and unsuspecting ones. Human sacrifices are done deep in the forest and up in the mountain caves, all in the name of Lord Bubi. Children are preferred in these blood sacrifices by the witches of dark magic and children with albinism are the most prized as there is a belief that immortality will be gained in the everlasting life through drinking their blood and cutting certain body parts to make foul medicine.

The ancients say that it is a disservice to conceal the light and contest its expansion in revealing more wonders of life. The echoes from the past reveal that it is through transcending the duality of positive and negative that one gains wisdom; it is a surrendered state of power that opens the book of life and amplifies the god-self. The children of the star surf the furthest frontiers of the halo produced by the spark of light. They roam unchartered terrains revealing the light in the dark world. They risk it all in the godforsaken territories to expose the absolute truth of all eternity.

An unnecessary war has been waged by Lord Bubi and his band of spirits for all eternity to deny what is; contradicting the movement of the natural order and disturbing the course of life. The knowing ones say that the friction between the upper world and underworld is part of the divine game created by all that is and absolute unity will prevail to straighten the 'madness' in the natural kingdom.

These are the legends told to generation upon generation of the young ones who sit with keen interest around the open fires across the vast land; swallowed in the moment and paying attention with glistening virgin eyes; listening to the wise ones sharing the knowledge of yore and the wisdom of the tribes that has stood the test of time.

Eight

THE MIDWIFE SUDDENLY woke up from the nightmare; she was soaking wet and her heart skipped a beat, pounding from the undesirable vision she had seen before her. The revelations were hard to believe.

'How could this be?' she silently thought.

'The albino baby died on that rainy day,' the midwife mumbled under her breath.

She paced the room, wondering and decoding how it came to be that the shameful infant survived the drowning. Her mind took her back to that eventful day. Images of her throwing the infant down the mighty Mfolozi River as the biological mother looked on teary-eyed were revealed.

She contemplated whether the high priest of darkness was playing tricks on her for his own amusement. The high priest, Mpundulu, is known for his wicked sense of humour; she earnestly wished that it was him manipulating her dreams with undesirable 'falsehood'. Sleep seduced her to the world of dreams yet again and she saw the girl child. She had grown into a delightful maiden. The midwife tossed and turned as the nightmare haunted her living soul. She woke up and beads of sweat ran down the lines of her wrinkled face. The dream not only revealed that she was living; she seemed to be thriving in the distant lands.

The midwife was dumbfounded and unable to comprehend how the baby survived the drowning. She was confused as to how to cut the Gordian knot presented to her. She continued pacing up and down the room, mumbling under her breath. This could mean trouble.

'She should have died that day.' The thought came back to her over and over.

She took a bottle of a foul medicine from under the table and took two sips of the dark potion. She rinsed her mouth out over and over and stepped outside, spitting and cursing the living day of the albino child. She looked up into the sky in the darkest hour of the morning as if looking for an omen to untangle the riddle. She spoke in twisted tongues, summoning the lord of darkness, Lord Bubi, to come to her aid and guide her.

'Oh lord of darkness, the ruler of the vast land, ruler of the known and unknown world, the one who is and ever was; I plead to you my lord, please untangle the undesirable mystery hanging over my head,' she begged him on her knees.

The dream troubled the midwife as it meant that she had failed in her duty, and her wishes to be crowned as a high priestess one day in the world of dark spirits would be in jeopardy. She took a dried-out dead tortoise that was next to the altar on a reed mat and broke off its head before grinding it on a stone until it turned powdery. She sniffed the powder and sneezed forcefully. She cursed the albino girl with venom.

'Death will visit you one of these days, you defiled ghost of a child,' she cursed.

'Your days are numbered; mark my words!' she yelled with anger.

She was determined to set things straight and went deep into the great forest of Nyavini before the break of dawn. The dense forest has witnessed its fair share of darkest horrors serving in the name of Lord Bubi. It has seen many human sacrifices and dark rituals performed by witches of dark magic. No ordinary person dares to enter the mouth of this forbidden forest.

The sparkling river of stars moved further and further away in the early morning hour as she went deeper in the unventured territory. She crossed many streams and went up and down the hills with purpose in her stride. The hooting owls looked at her curiously; her mind was full with obscure thoughts. She reached the mouth of the great forest at a perfect time, when the creatures of the night were taking rest and the day creatures were preparing to wake up. She crawled underneath the dense fog and went deep into the forest. The serene smell and sounds of the forest greeted her but she paid little attention to them as her mission became all-consuming. Morning birds announced the dawn of the new day but she remained oblivious to them as she was single-minded in her pursuit.

She went further and deeper into territories that few dare to tread. Uneasiness settled on her old and weathered shoulders. Light struggled to penetrate the densely tree-populated area. She was looking for a specific type of herb to be picked while there was still heavy dew. This sacred herb is very rare in the vast land. The herb with divine powers 'sleeps' during the day and comes alive in the still of the night, and is at its peak before the dawn of day. The midwife found the herb in the damp soil, dug it up and pulled it out by its roots, where its power lies. She dug out a few before making her way back home, anxious for preparation.

As soon as she got home, she ground up the thick roots of the herb on a stone and cooked the powder in a small three-legged cast-iron pot. She mumbled as she stirred the medicine.

'Reveal this ghost of a child, oh lord of lords! Show me where she is, oh lord of darkness and I promise to deliver death to her unsuspecting soul.'

The medicine is able to transport the dream-self to all

the places the dreamer wishes to visit and gives more freedom to the roaming spirit. Once the medicine is drunk, sleep calls in an infectious hum and the physical actuality begins to collapse; the dream-self is then awakened and the spirit becomes one with the wind reaching all the corners of the known and unknown world.

The midwife stared at the wall inside the hut thinking over the events of the morning and planning her next move. She wondered whether the biological mother knew that the albino child was living happily in the distant lands; it had been a while since the midwife had seen her. The last time she had heard of the mother had been via the village rumour mill. There were stories that she was losing her mind and that she spent a lot of time alone locked in her unmaintained homestead. Her husband had long left her for another woman. The midwife undertook to visit her on the morrow.

The medicine boiled and exuded foam. The steam gave off a unique spicy scent in the hut. The midwife lifted the cast-iron pot off the fire after the liquid had simmered and poured the medicine into an enamel pot for it to cool down before bottling it. She took dried and powdered monkey brain, wild mouse and snake, and mixed them with the care of a seasoned practitioner.

She believed that the monkey brain gives her vigilance and the wild mouse made her avoid being easily detectable, while the snake provided her with a killer instinct. In the African spiritual perspective, the knowing ones use not only the genetic information that is found in the cell nuclei of living organisms but also take into cognisance the consciousness and spirit it carries.

She sprinkled the mix of the powdered medicine on the back of her left hand and licked it. She took a spoon of the medicine and added two drops of water to the powder to make it moist. She smeared the paste behind her ears, on her eyebrows, the back of her neck and behind her knees. She also believed that the medicine enabled her to see the future as clearly as she could see the past; believing is reality.

Evening came and darkness fell. The old wise ones say that night is for passion and desire; it is also for fanaticism and shady dealings. It's when the most gentle, genuine and suppressed sides come out to play under the non-judgmental eyes of the stars. The midwife evoked the spirits of darkness to protect her. She sprinkled liquid medicine around the hut and its entrance to chase away unwanted spirits.

'Go away you impure spirits. Go away you diabolic spirits and burn in the scorching fires of forever-night,' she cursed.

She then took a foul dark potion and rinsed her mouth out with it before going outside, spitting and cursing the very day the spark of light lit the darkness.

'Reign for all eternity, oh lord of darkness. I bow to you Lord Bubi; the one who stares at fear and makes it run for the hills.' She bellowed the chant with deep passion.

She looked around for any prying eyes before going back inside the hut. She undressed and smeared her whole body with porcupine fat to fight off unwanted dreams. She sang ritual songs usually chanted in special ceremonies by those of dark magic. She then took a sip from the magic herb of dreams and slept soundly for the first time in a while. There were no nightmares haunting her living soul. The herb crystallised the vision of her all-knowing eye and she travelled far and wide to the distant lands in search of the albino child. She went looking in different homesteads in the different villages across the hills and the plains. The midnight hour passed as she searched the unsuspecting sleeping villages. The darkest hour of the morning heightened the mood and finally her spirit was called to look for the homestead of a traditional healer in the village of Dingilizwe and she was then drawn to the homestead where the unsuspecting albino child slept. She circled her as she slept and showered her with vile intentions. The albino child tossed and turned, trying to break away from the spell. The spirit of the midwife sat on her chest and she was unable to move. The albino girl mumbled in her sleep in an attempt to break the bond of the nightmare. She kicked and screamed and eventually woke everyone up in the hut. A candle was lit and the spirit of the midwife escaped into the darkest hour of the morning.

The roaming spirit of the midwife descended back to her body and she woke up. The first part of her mission was achieved. She lit a bundle of spicy-smelling dry leaves and knelt; she began to pray and thanked Lord Bubi for guiding her on her night-time journey.

'Thank you, oh lord of lords. Thank you for revelations, my lord. I promise to deliver death to her undeserving soul.' She made a pact.

She stood up and pondered her next step. She dressed warmly and was out of the door before the break of dawn on her way to see the biological mother and tell her the new and disturbing revelations.

Nine

The biological mother walked on the road and the road turned into a peculiar gigantic repulsive creature with a drooping mouth and fiery eyes. The monster seemed of another world and belonged in the deepest depths of the underworld. The creature had many arms, like an octopus, and devoured everything in its path as it moved. It roared mightily and fantastically, swallowing every sound in the known world. A flying crocodile with menacing eyes surveyed the night sky with vigilance. She hid behind the trunk of a tree and the tree turned into a snake with thirteen heads. The snake hissed and spat at her with balls of fire and she ran as fast as she could into the sleeping village nearby. She found a homestead with three huts overlooking a mountain on the outskirts of the village and burst into the main hut seeking help. She was breathing heavily with cold fear written across her face and to her amazement and disgust, she saw the high priest, Mpundulu, fondling sleeping young boys in the hut. She wanted to wake up from the nightmare but her body was paralysed. She tossed and turned wanting to escape the underworld but the nightmare arrested the dream-self, refusing to let her go.

'Wake up, wake up!' The midwife shook her out of the nightmare.

She screamed a piercing shriek. She was drenched in sweat and her body was shaking.

'Listen to me you wretched commoner, that despicable baby of yours didn't die that day.' The midwife snapped at her to bring her back to the apparent actuality.

Nokwakha looked at her, lost and dumbfounded, wondering how the midwife came to be in her hut. The midwife scooped water from a bucket underneath the table and splashed her face.

'Ahhh! What the hell are you doing?' Nokwakha screamed at the midwife.

'Shut up you sorry excuse of a human being!' The midwife cut the mood with a wicked harsh tone.

Nokwakha was quiet in an instant and stared at the menacing figure in front of her. The evil eyes of the midwife sent an icy chill up her spine.

'The albino child did not die that day,' the midwife broke the news.

Nokwakha collapsed like a boneless creature and fainted the instant she heard the statement.

'What the hell! You son of a double-sexed goat!' the midwife screeched.

Nokwakha lay on the ground, unresponsive to the name-calling. The midwife shook her violently but she remained indifferent to her efforts.

'Wake up!' She shook her once again.

Nokwakha was lost in a world beyond and seemed out of breath. The midwife splashed her with water once again and she gasped for air. She began spewing out unstructured sentences and was making no sense. She spoke in tongues as if possessed by alien spirits. She was deranged and overwhelmed by madness.

'Nokwakha!' The midwife yelled at her by name in frustration.

She didn't respond and continued speaking the jumbled

language of a mad person, ignoring the midwife. The midwife slapped her but she continued churning out incoherent words as if nothing had happened. Nokwakha looked right through the midwife with no acknowledgement of her presence. The midwife became restless and irritated by the whole episode and was helpless in rescuing the situation to normality.

'I want my child.' Suddenly Nokwakha spoke some sense.

Relief ran through the veins of the midwife.

'I want my child,' Nokwakha repeated her request.

'We have to make a plan to get to her and finish the job undone,' said the midwife with coldness in her voice.

'I want my child,' Nokwakha echoed the words once again.

The midwife realised that sanity hadn't actually prevailed as Nokwakha kept repeating the same sentence like a chorus, over and over. The midwife changed the abrasive tone towards Nokwakha and calmed the situation. She was determined to get Nokwakha on her side and was willing to use trickery to get what she wanted. She tenderly cared for her and begged for sanity to reign.

'I want my child,' Nokwakha mumbled once more.

'Ssshhh, it's going to be okay.' The midwife offered her assurance. 'Lie down and rest for a while,' the midwife persuaded Nokwakha.

Nokwakha didn't respond and kept repeating the chorus of the emotion deep within.

'Lie down; it's going to be okay,' the midwife insisted.

'Ssshhh, trust me; lean on me, we'll find your daughter, I promise.' She stroked the emotional tender sides of Nokwakha.

Nokwakha finally heeded the appeal and slept. The ancients say that when days are dark, friends are few; Nokwakha could attest to the trueness of this ancient proverb. The midwife managed to deceive her into believing that she was that friend who would relieve her paining heart. She was blind in her desperation and was tricked by the midwife. It was all about self-preservation from the midwife's perspective and her blackened heart cared less in actuality.

Nokwakha was seduced to a world of pure dreams and slept like a little child. She was exhausted from the recurring nightmares that drained her life force and kept her awake in the darkest hours. The midwife got up and contemplated different conspiracies; her mind was flooded with wicked thoughts. There was still the unfinished pursuit of delivering death to the albino girl. It was important to her that Nokwakha participate in her quest and also be initiated into the world of dark spirits.

Dusk fell upon the vast land and the midwife woke Nokwakha up. She woozily opened her eyes and they met the unflinching stare of the midwife.

'We have to go,' the midwife said gently.

'I can't leave you here alone; dress warmly,' said the midwife with false concern.

Nokwakha put trust in her and soon thereafter they were on their way under the non-judgemental stars to the homestead of the midwife.

Ten

NOKWAKHA IS A HAUNTED woman. Guilt has followed her like a dreadful shadow since that awful day at the Mfolozi River. She tried to shake off the despicable act by suppressing it in her memory bank but without success. The wise ones usually say that no evil deed remains unpunished and Nokwakha could testify to that. She stayed awake at night to run away from the nightmares that visited her in the dark hours. There were those who were suspicious of her story that the baby was stillborn. The lies troubled her living soul. She couldn't sleep at night without hearing the desperate cry of her child seeking a mother's love. She tried to have another baby with her husband in an attempt to replace her but could not fall pregnant again. She frequented village herbalists to induce her to flower and bear another child but all was in vain. She begged her husband who was losing patience and wanting to leave her as he was obsessed with having an heir to his legacy. The husband eventually left her and married another woman in the village. She was taunted and jeered at by the other women because of her infertility. The gossip weighed on her over time and she became a recluse.

They arrive at the homestead of the midwife in the still of the night. The midwife lights a candle and surveys the room. She takes a reed mat from the north end of the room and offers Nokwakha something to sit on. There is a heavy silence in the hut.

'You need cleansing to clear all the unwanted energy in your midst,' says the midwife.

Nokwakha doesn't respond; the midwife prepares a fire in the middle of the hut and cooks the medicine. She whispers under her breath as she stirs the liquid remedy.

'This is for you to steam your whole body,' she says to Nokwakha.

The midwife lights incense and takes a blanket hanging on a string on the left side of the circling interior wall and gives it to Nokwakha.

'The water is about to boil now; take off your clothes,' she instructs.

Nokwakha takes off her clothes and covers her body with the blanket. The midwife pours the boiling medicine in the washbasin.

'Cover the steam under your blanket quickly,' she tells Nokwakha.

Nokwakha kneels, bends over the washbasin and covers the steam with the blanket.

'The vapour is burning,' says Nokwakha in displeasure.

'Stay put; don't let the steam escape,' bellows the midwife.

'But I'm burning,' she protests.

'Keep quiet and stop complaining, the medicine will lose its power.'

'But ...'

'Ssshhh,' the midwife interjects.

The midwife murmurs a song and moves around the hut in a rhythm. She takes two sticks and a drum hanging on the wall and beats it with an almost concealed sound. She circles Nokwakha a few times. She prays silently to the archangels of the underworld in the hidden recess of all things dark. She sings once again a song usually sung at special ceremonies by those of dark magic and suddenly cuts the song abruptly.

'You can come out now,' says the midwife.

Nokwakha lifts the blanket and is dripping with sweat.

'Go outside and wash your body with the medicine and let the wind caress you,' the midwife tells her.

Nokwakha pours water into the medicine to cool it down and goes outside under the jewel sky. She washes her whole body and feels lighter. There is a sudden spring in her step. She is blind to the real intentions of the midwife. She doesn't recognise that she is already in the process of being initiated into the world of the dark spirits.

'Don't overstay outside, the evening wind has a cold bite,' shouts the midwife from the inside of the hut.

Nokwakha steps inside in an instant.

'How are you feeling?' asks the midwife.

'Refreshed; I can feel my pores breathing,' says Nokwakha.

'Good; I had to clear the veil of bad luck surrounding your aura.'

The midwife gives her a powdered medicine to sniff; it makes her sneeze.

'Heeeeetuuu! Heeeeetuuu! What is this thing you've made me sniff?' she asks.

'Heeeeetuuu!' she sneezes yet again.

The midwife doesn't dignify the question with any acknowledgement.

'Here, butter your body with this.' The midwife gives her the porcupine fat.

Nokwakha smears the fat on her body. The midwife lights dry leaves that induce drowsiness and Nokwakha is seduced by sleep to its temple.

'Lie down, I'm coming back,' says the midwife.

Nokwakha is soon asleep and the midwife is out the door into the still of the night.

The midwife was once a noble servant of the tribes and revered in all the land. She has travelled far and wide delivering the babies of commoners and royals alike and is held in high regard by all. Even when there was a battle among the tribes, she went about her work without being molested by any of the warring groups.

She's wise and clairvoyant but has remained an enigma all her working life. She has a gift of sensing and seeing the life journey of the newborns before they take their first steps in the thorny plains of life and she shares her visions with the mothers and an appropriate name is given to the infant as a reminder of their purpose. This is important to the new mothers as the tribes believe that one's name should act as a compass in the journey of life.

Over a period of time, the midwife noticed that there were special souls being born across the land; babies that had old souls and an incredible awareness of what is. These children were in some way handicapped for reasons she couldn't comprehend. Some couldn't speak properly and had difficulty in communicating verbally. Others were deaf and some were blind; they were born as outcasts but had an uncanny ability to see things that others couldn't see. She noticed that these divine powers were more endowed in children with albinism. These children didn't necessarily preach good over evil but sang songs of enchantment with their hearts. Their magical spiritual works were unseen; however, change was happening as a result of them being born.

The lord of darkness became aware of this phenomenon of these indigo children and contrived a cunning plan to extinguish their light. The ultimate plan of Lord Bubi's from time immemorial was to hijack and corrupt points of entry to the different worlds, and the course of birth was such a point of entrance that needed to be manipulated. He assigned the high priestess Mthakathi to corrupt the midwife so that such babies were killed at birth to rid the kingdom of the threat they may pose.

The high priestess of darkness appeared in the midwife's dreams a number of times, draining her of all the characteristics that were intended for spiritual ascension, and managed to convince her to serve the underworld. She used black magic to manipulate and infringe upon the midwife's free will. The midwife was promised to serve as a high priestess of the underworld upon fulfilling her earthly mission. Mthakathi warned the midwife of a girl with albinism that would be born in the first moon of spring. She foresaw the birth of Nwelezelanga; legends of the tribes foretold her coming and there were many children of the star who paved the way. The stage was finally set when she was born but the dark worshippers had clandestine and immoral plans to contradict what is; Mthakathi told the midwife to deliver death to Nwelezelanga's undeserving soul as the child would go on to make 'false promises' to the masses about everlasting life and disturb the old order of the wicked empire.

The midwife chose to act as a guardian for Lord Bubi by killing babies with extraordinary awareness and deceiving their mothers by telling them that they either had had a miscarriage, or given birth to stillborn babies. Those who managed to survive were deemed as cursed and killed soon thereafter. The midwife chose to descend to the lower ranks of the underworld and served the world of suffering and black magic.

The night was restless, the clouds moved hesitantly in the sky and the wind hummed a troubled tune full of obscure messages. The midwife carried a sack on her back and moved with purpose. Nokwakha was behind her with eyes full of wonder. Dogs howled curiously at the moon and haunted the evening. The two night explorers went beyond the sleeping villages and deep into the woods. Owls hooted from the tall trees and bats flew surprisingly close above their heads. They entered the notorious enigmatic Nyavini forest. The midwife waited for Nokwakha, who was trailing behind.

'Follow closely behind me and be cautious where you're stepping,' said the midwife.

The unknown observed from behind the bushes and the creatures of the night whistled curious melodies. The women went deeper into the forest, passed some streams and then reached a bare patch of land next to a big rock.

'Let's collect dry wood to make a fire,' instructed the midwife.

They collected wood, which was readily available, and the midwife made a bonfire that reached for the sky. She took a bottle with a liquid concoction from her pouch and gave it to Nokwakha to drink.

'This will help you to relax a bit and transport you to higher planes,' the midwife assured her.

Nokwakha took a sip and she frowned in reaction to the unpleasant taste of the drink.

'Drink some more!' bellowed the midwife.

Nokwakha took a couple of sips and gave the bottle back to the midwife, who gulped some of it down.

The midwife then took off her clothes and painted her body with ochre. She took a hideous mask and a flamboyant headdress from her sack and put them on. She started to sing from the base of her gut and danced around the bonfire in dizzy circles. She made grunting and shrieking sounds. She was drunk with emotions and high in spirit.

Nokwakha looked on hypnotised and bewildered by the activities. The midwife leapt over the fire and made horse sounds. She spoke in tongues, summoning the spirit of Lord Bubi, and foam formed in the corners of her mouth.

'Take off your clothes,' the midwife roared and took a razor from her pouch. 'You need protection from bad omens that keep attaching themselves to you.'

She made tiny razor incisions all over Nokwakha's body and smeared powdered medicine into the cuts. Nokwakha was blind to the thickening plot. The midwife gave Nokwakha another sip of the liquid concoction.

'Stand up,' instructed the midwife.

'Follow me,' she shouted.

They circled the fire; the liquid potion stirred up happy emotions and they laughed deliriously and danced crazily. Nokwakha was mesmerised under the spell of the midwife and had completely forfeited her will. They jumped over the bonfire and the flames caressed their naked bodies. Characteristics of a wild animal had taken over. The midwife then took a kitten from her sack and decapitated it. She drank the dripping blood and smeared her whole body with it. She made Nokwakha suck the blood of the lifeless creature and also smeared her body with blood. The midwife ripped and tore the lifeless kitten into pieces and swallowed the raw meat; she gave Nokwakha her own share to swallow. A scream echoed in the dark forest.

'Can you hear that?' enquired the unknowing apprentice with glistening eyes.

'Here, wear this.' The midwife gave Nokwakha a black-hooded robe and put one on herself.

Nokwakha was a lost soul in the deep territory of all things dark. The scream got louder and louder. Two masked figures appeared from the bushes dragging an albino child. The child kicked and screamed for dear life. The shrill cry arrested the night. Nokwakha looked on in shock. The midwife bowed at the two masked figures; there was mutual respect among them. The midwife assisted them in tying the girl's hands and feet with rope. One of the masked women started to beat a small drum and the booming sound echoed in the still of the night, reaching the deeper terrains of the forest. They danced with rhythm and the midwife joined the festivities. Nokwakha joined them and danced awkwardly, showing hesitation. The hold of the liquid potion she drank earlier was wearing off.

The ritual reached its climax as the group feverishly chanted songs of praise to Lord Bubi. They paid tribute to the dark star in the hidden recess of outer space. They called upon the spirit of Mpundulu and Mthakathi to appear in their midst. The midwife fed more wood to the fire. The masked women jumped over the flames and giggled, like a cackle of hyenas. The midwife sharpened a knife for Nokwakha to do the honours of the sacrifice and the masked women dragged the albino girl closer to the fire. One of the women took a burning stick and burnt the little feet of the girl. She screamed a deafening cry and a chorus of evil laughter cascaded from the congregation. Nokwakha was terrified and dumbstruck. The worshippers of darkness fed upon the agony the girl was experiencing; the dark spirits thrive in the disharmony and pain of others. They called upon the dark lord.

'Oh lord of darkness, ruler of eternity, we bow to you in all humbleness.'

'Welcome to your kingdom another servant to your rule.'

'With this sacrifice, we ask that you accept Nokwakha as one of your own.'

The midwife gave Nokwakha the knife. The two masked women untied the girl, held her tightly and presented her for the sacrifice.

'Slit her throat,' instructed the midwife.

Nokwakha was shaken and cold fear rendered her body in complete spasm. The deepest self didn't want to partake in the evil ceremony any longer. She saw through the manipulations of the midwife as no soul remains forever ignorant. Without warning, she started sprinting away. The midwife and the two masked women were caught off guard and slow to react. They realised that Nokwakha was abandoning the ceremony and the midwife was in hot pursuit in no time. The masked women wrestled with the wailing child in an attempt to tie her with the rope in order to assist with the chase. Nokwakha increased the distance between her and her pursuers and ran for her life. She ran through untamed bushes and picked up thorns along the way; however, all was secondary to survival. She ran like a woman possessed. The midwife was not as fast, but she made up for her shortcoming with her unmatched stamina and she also knew the landscape of the forest intimately. The two soon lost the masked women and crossed many streams. It was a cat-and-mouse chase. Nokwakha left a trail of disturbed bushes that made it easy for the midwife to track her. The forest was alive with suspense. The midwife was determined to catch Nokwakha and to will undignified death to the 'traitor of the highest order'; this wasn't only a humiliation to her but a disgrace to the mighty dark lord. Nokwakha never looked back and only concentrated on getting out of the midwife's sight forever. She was introduced to a new kind of fear. The sheer terror of being caught gave her the energy she needed. She ruffled bushes and frightened rabbits, impalas and other sleeping creatures of the wild.

She reached yet another stream and stopped to quench her elephant thirst. She rested behind a big rock; her heart skipped a beat as anxiety overwhelmed her. She peeped from behind the rock, scoping for her pursuer but the midwife was nowhere to be found. She was startled by a bristling sound from the bush behind her when a gazelle suddenly jumped out and galloped up the hill. She was paralysed with shock. She scoped her surrounds yet again and there was calm in the natural kingdom. She rested, believing she had done enough to lose the midwife. She began to take out the thorns she had picked up along the way. The non-judgemental stars sparkled and rejoiced in exhibition of the natural splendour. She was dripping with sweat and welcomed the breeze that fanned and cooled her. The changing winds brought heavy dark clouds and suddenly the midwife appeared in the distance. She paced slowly and surveyed the area with hawk eyes. There was determination in her stride and the stamina of an ostrich in her legs. She crossed the stream and looked on the ground for Nokwakha's footprints but they disappeared near the rocky surface. The midwife continued up the hill but had a change of heart after a few steps. She sensed something in the air; a seasoned predator, her instincts were as sharp as a cheetah's. Nokwakha looked on from behind the corner of the big oval rock, pleading with the gods to blind the midwife of her exact location. The midwife turned back and started looking behind the many rocks next to the stream. She was edging closer to her and Nokwakha was petrified. She jumped out from behind the rock and ran as fast as she could away from the midwife. The midwife was hot on her trail with much more zeal in her demeanour; there was surety in her heart that she was going to capture Nokwakha. The all-knowing heavens watched yet another earthly episode. Nokwakha was getting tired and kept looking behind her at frequent intervals. She took a wrong path as a result and it steered her to a dead end in the gigantic cliff. She was dumbstruck when she reached the mount with nowhere to go. The midwife closed in on her and Nokwakha thought of jumping off the cliff. She stood on the edge of the cliff, paralysed and unclear of what to do next. The midwife approached and flashed her a crooked smile.

'You thought you could outrun me? Hahahaha! Keep dreaming. Do you know the disgrace you've caused me? Do you?' she roared.

Nokwakha was silent. She was breathing heavily and almost swallowed her tongue as the cold fear overwhelmed her. The midwife stepped closer towards her. Nokwakha had no space to manoeuvre; she either had to fight or flee down the slope. She threw herself to the battle of doom; only one of them was going to live to tell the tale. They locked eyes for a moment without anyone giving an inch. They fell on the ground with a big thud and wrestled on the ground, with the midwife seemingly having the upper hand. Nokwakha was desperate to free herself from the clutches of the midwife but she held her firm and didn't let go. The midwife twisted Nokwakha's arm and locked her into submission. Nokwakha screamed as a result of the unbearable pain but the midwife tightened her grip even harder.

'You're breaking my arm!' Nokwakha screamed in agony.

Her cries fell on deaf ears.

'Aaahhh!' she screamed again.

Out of pure desperation Nokwakha lifted the midwife with an incredible force she never knew existed within her. The midwife held her firm, refusing to let go. Nokwakha bit her and the midwife released her grip. She then pushed her in an attempt to escape and the midwife fell down the cliff to her death. Nokwakha fell to the ground in utter exhaustion and relief ran through her veins.

The moon echoed songs of wonder, full of mystical undertones.

Eleven

THE NIGHT WAS HAUNTED by wicked spirits. It was that time of the evening when the negative stimuli in the atmosphere are heightened and the fanatics of the dark world come out to play. The mood suffocated her existence; Nokwakha stood on the edge of the cliff, wanting to end all her misery. Her heart was heavy with suicidal intentions. She was lost in the valley of the shadow of death. Life had been one everlasting nightmare. She had forsaken all reason to live yet another day. Her heart was weathered by impious storms; pain had followed her like a taunting relentless nemesis throughout this thing called life.

She wanted to end it all but fear inexplicably still had a hold of her. Death stood proud from beyond, wooing her to take the plunge into her embrace. The spark of light deep in her soul fought for attention. She couldn't master absolute courage to will death to her tortured self. She walked and walked along the cliff with obscure thoughts hanging on the edge of her imagination. The dark cloud of gloom hovered above her.

She was overwhelmed by feelings that reminded her of her daughter. She wondered much about her and what would have happened if she had never listened to the midwife. Tears fell down her face. She was utterly broken. She yearned to be reunited with her daughter even if it was for one moment. She was curious to see the kind of person she had become; it was all a dream. She reached out for her in the deep corridors of pure dreams asking for forgiveness.

'Oh daughter of mine, I am such a shame and disgrace to you and all humanity. What right do I even have to call you my daughter? I'm definitely not a mother but a monster that devours her own young; I could never justify my demonic act in my attempt to rob you the magnificence of life.'

Rays of light began to protrude on the faraway horizon; Nokwakha communicated the feelings deep within to the living ether, pleading for forgiveness from her daughter and to the divine spirits that roam the land. She wanted to be relieved of the pain she had had to carry ever since that horrific day.

'Forgive me almighty Qamata for I have sinned; words feel inadequate in expressing my soul's intentions. I surrender to your might, oh all-knowing one, and offer my soul as a sacrifice for the greater good; I am open and willing for justice to be served in retribution for my actions.'

She begged for forgiveness to the lord of day and night, the lord of the upper world and underworld, the lord of the known and unknown world; tears continued to stream down her face. The dancing sun rose ignorant to the earthly episode; it served yet another day, giving light to the known world. Nokwakha was lost in hopelessness. She flirted with death and the desire to take her own life became stronger. She convinced herself that death would bring peace and an eternal resting place. She was ignorant to the fact that a soul cannot be annihilated and the false idea of suicide would actually impede the development of her soul and intensify the guilt in another world as past lives are not disconnected to the present and future selves. She was drunk with depression and completely rejected her tortured existence. She was dead inside.

Part Three

Twelve

'WHEN YOU ASK FOR a "sign", know that the need for a "sign" to avail itself is already a "sign"," says Nomkhubulwana as we sit on top of a giant precipice of the Mojaji mountain overlooking the distant lands.

The mood has been heavy and brooding since our great trek earlier that morning. Nomkhubulwana has showered me with wisdom, filling my cup from her overflowing knowledge about the book of life.

'I have walked on these thorny plains of this ungrateful earth and surfed the deepest wells of being; my mission is now fulfilled, I won't stay any longer as those in the land of the spirit call with a definite voice,' she says in a low solemn tone.

'One of these mornings I will be gone; I dream of faraway lands where simplicity and purity reign supreme. I dream of the land beyond, the land of origins; the urge to be completely spirit overwhelms.' She reveals the dawning knowledge.

I listen while holding my breath; the glaring light exuding from her being mesmerises.

'Nwelezelanga, let other souls heal from the spirit that you are, my child.'

She shares yet another pearl of wisdom.

I let it all sink into my heart of hearts without any

filter; her very being swallows all of me in one enormous magical moment.

'You are like a shooting star that appears without notice and disappears without trace. You made a promise in your great ceremony to the wise spirits, before your earth-shattering birth, not to stay a while longer in the land of the walking dead. And like a shooting star you will vanish as quickly as you came.' She serves the abstract message.

'What do you mean?' I lean forward with curiosity.

'All will be revealed in due course, my child; I'm too forward and speaking out of turn. I should let you discover the secrets of your heart.' She keeps me in suspense.

'But you've whet my appetite already,' I protest.

'Look deep within; your greatest answers lie deep in the well of your soul sphere.'

A stony silence follows thereafter.

Nomkhubulwana lights impepho and kneels, over-looking the gigantic cliff, she lifts her hands high above her head and amazing grace exudes from her being. I follow her lead.

'Qamata!' The sound of her voice ricochets in the mountain.

'Mvelinqangi!'

'Oh great Nkulunkulu, please hear me almighty; the one who is and ever was.' Her voice echoes in the mountain gorge again and again.

She takes a deep breath before letting the feelings deep within fly with the wind. She prays loudly: 'Oh wandering souls of the land bound with the wind, surfing the furthest dreams; oh passionate hearts of the seas, welcoming of all the streams in your eloquent stride that breathes the very life; oh spirit of all spirits hidden behind the ten gates of eternity with all the knowing of the known world; fly away with thee to the seven corners of time and reveal thee to thy self; strip all the human fallibility and unmask the naked beauty that resides deep in all ages; unbound the earthly form that stands as obstacle to all purity; burn thy anxiety in the scorching flames of forever-night that know no end; sculpt a philosopher's stone with this very heart and bring upon a sage with crystallised purpose; fashion wings to thy soul and dare it to fly a pathless journey; swallow thee you blinding light; swallow thee you boundless love. Amen.'

Tears fall down the lines of her wizened face. Her eyes tell many stories. I am sensitive to the deeper truth she's expressing.

'My time is nigh, this is the moment of alchemy and the gods are in cahoots; I cannot overstay my welcome.' She shares the deeper truth.

She looks at me with eyes that hypnotise and penetrate my soul.

'My child, the world is turning; the seasons are changing. The volcanoes are erupting; the quakes are rumbling. The rains are flooding; the thundering storms roar with anger. The natural kingdom groans in pangs. The world of spirits speaks profoundly. The council of high spirits from the inexplicable world of paramount earth is becoming anxious. Messages of warning are communicated every so often but fall on deaf ears. The children of the star are sent to pass messages from beyond and their messages are met with ridicule at times and indifference most of the time.'

My heart gets fuller with a muddle of emotions and the breath dances into a different rhythm. Stories of yore are awakened. There's much more to discover; surrender is necessary.

'Be the light, my child; let your spirit be felt in its purest,' she says to me and her eyes once again bore into my soul.

'Open your heart bare and let the divine inspire; bow in all humbleness.' She feeds me the deep passion in her spirit.

'I will continue to walk by your side; we journey this road together and are bound by something deeper than both of us. Our history is written in the stars,' she assures me.

I listen attentively with the ears of my soul. Nomkhubulwana divulges the knowledge of time past and greater truths from beyond. She expresses her readiness to journey to higher planes and prepares me for my journey.

She's bare and open, sharing for the better. She delivers yet another sermon for the soul.

'Awaken your god-given spirit my child; free your mind from the world of form and become a partner in creation by refining the original spirit. Focus within and experience the highest kingdoms, the heaven of the heart and the mysterious openings to ancestral realms. By focusing within, the energies of the body increase and the light crystallises, thus achieving spiritual illumination. Persist with inward focus and the fire of spirit will be ignited and thus sagehood will be bestowed by the higher forces; it is through pure effort of concentration that the spirit alchemises and you'll arrive at the effortless. When you preserve the original spirit, you will experience life outside the duality of positive and negative and therefore transcend the "world".

'Let not the physical actuality grab your absolute focus as, in doing so, there'll be running unguarded leakage of original spirit. Always remember that the light is within and the absolute unified energy of celestial immortals resides in the deepest depths of the soul sphere. You are the master of your destiny; all the predestined dreams await for you to put much more emotion in them to make them dense and they shall appear in your apparent reality.'

The sermon of the transcendent message speaks directly with my original self. I feel lightness in my being. The channels to the deeper self are wide open as the message moves from shallow to deep and from crude to fine. Heavy dark clouds gather in the distance and move above the majestic mountain; forked lightning flashes and big raindrops begin to fall. We seek refuge in a cave and listen to the mighty roar of the heavens in exhibition of divine power. The thunderstorm doesn't last long; the rainbow paints the horizon with magical undertones. We slowly make our way down the slopes on our journey back home.

The red soil breathes new life as the butterflies flaunt refreshing innocence.

Thirteen

THE SUN RISES EAGERLY and the birds sing beautifully, praising the dawn of the new day. The recent heavy rains have thoroughly nourished the maize fields and filled up the rivers. Spring has sprung and the natural kingdom blossoms in absolute splendour. We sit lazily in the big hut listening to Mama's tales about the 'good old golden days' while doing beadwork.

Mama comes from a long ancestry of traditional healers and noble medicine men. She has been taught the ways of the forefathers and foremothers on how to relate to and heal the mind, body and spirit. She tells us that this is not the life that she chose but rather the life that chose her. She knows a lot about plants and their healing powers and says that from the African spiritual perspective we don't only relate to the genetic material of the plants but also their consciousness and spirit.

I've observed that when she consults with people she goes beyond the physical body and heals the energy field of the individual by balancing their vibrations. Sometimes she burns impepho, sage or other ritual incense to alter consciousness and energy to calm the physical body of the individual and at times she uses medicine that doesn't talk directly to the physical ailment but rather shocks the sense of taste, and therefore the psyche, and this has an effect in altering consciousness which then heals the body holistically. At times I've seen her use detoxification techniques to clear density in the physical body by steaming patients with certain herbs or giving them medicine to purge their bowels, rid phlegm in their chest and any unwanted waste that brings about blockage in their physical system. She puts prominence in the spiritual perspective though, and treats the physical focus as secondary reality. She always tells her patients not to overemphasise their physical focus as that may be limiting; she says when one becomes dense like that, the extraterrestrial vision or existence is cut off and one then misses the bulk of the multilayered reality and god-self.

A middle-aged woman with a young girl enters the hut. Zimasa offers them a reed mat to sit on; their demeanour exudes humility but the woman's eyes give away her troubled soul and the girl's eyes looked dazed, as if in another world.

'Camagu,' Mama greets the visitors.

'Camagu Makhosi,' the mystified woman acknowledges the greeting.

'How are you?' Mama asks about their well-being.

'If all was well we'd be resting at home, Makhosi; we came here seeking your help,' says the woman with a heavy tone.

Mama lights impepho and puts it in front of her. She then lights a candle and asks the visitors to move closer to her at the north end of the room next to her altar.

'My child has been acting queerly for a while, Makhosi. She has become a wanderer and sometimes she leaves the homestead without notice and when we search for her we often find her on the banks of the Mthonyama River.' The woman shares her troubles.

'When we ask her why she's there she says an old woman in her dream told her to meet her there and when we ask the whereabouts of this woman she points to an empty space; she sees her but we can't. She has described the features of the old woman and the elders of the family are convinced that it's her great-grandmother.' The woman breathes heavily.

'When she is at home, she prefers to sleep with the goats in the shed. She also tells us about voices she hears that want her absolute attention. She hasn't been eating much lately and is becoming thin as a result,' says the mother in distress.

The young girl's eyes look disorientated. There are many like her who have been brought by their concerned families because of the perceived anomaly in their behaviour, those who see and feel 'things' that are not apparent in the physical actuality. Mama usually diagnoses with ease when there is a spiritual crisis that needs to be guided with absolute care.

Mama asks the young girl to lean forward and inhale the smoke of the everlasting plant. The girl inhales and coughs a few times. Mama sings a song and Zimasa grabs a drum hanging on the wall. Aunt Nontsebenzo and I follow suit, clapping and singing along to the haunting tune. Mama picks up her charmed cow-tail whisk from next to her and whips the air; she circles the hut in a rhythmic dance. The spirits rise with song and dance. Mama asks the girl to stand up and dance with her. The girl obliges and dances awkwardly. The booming drum talks with the matters of the heart. The girl suddenly throws herself on the floor and cries uncontrollably. She kicks and screams as the song is deliriously chanted. Mama takes the impepho and hovers the smoke closer to her nostrils. Mama repeatedly taps the girl lightly on her back and calls on the girl's ancestors to visit. The girl calms down a bit and Mama starts addressing her mother.

'Your child has a calling, ubizo; it's a solid yearning for a deep connection that transcends the apparent reality into the celestial realm. Rituals need to be done to aid the birth of the deeper self and allow the emerging thwasa to move out of the distress and accept the calling wholeheartedly by cooperating with ancestors in the healing work they want to express. There have been amathwasa who have stayed with us for some time in order to be trained as traditional healers.

'Your child is reaching out to higher paradigms, the spiritual realm of those of old. The suspect behaviour she has been exhibiting is an emergency call to be tuned to higher planes of the old wise ones from beyond. The ancestors use sensitive souls like her in an attempt to convey messages they want communicated to the land of the walking dead. The call is absolute and she has to be guided with care or imbalances may occur and sick energy may haunt her soul and psyche until such time that she honours the call from those of yesteryear.'

Mama takes her duty as a healer very seriously. She sees it as her most important calling to assist those who are ready to break through to the ancestral realm.

'Your daughter has been chosen as a medium by higher spirits to pass messages from the spirit realm to those who walk the unforgiving terrain and to all the troubled souls of the tribes. The old wise one that appears in her dreams and calls her to the river is an ancestral spirit that is rising and reaching out to her and the whole clan at large. She is appearing in her dreams to form a bond with your child so she can use her for spiritual ends.' Stillness fills the moment.

'The hallucinations and mind disturbances that you have observed are as a result of the ancestral spirit demanding to be heard; your daughter's longing for the connection with ancestral spirits has been unconscious but the ancestors have continued bombarding her with messages trusting that her sensitivity would finally make her yield to their call. It's a good thing that you came now because further spiritual imbalances would have occurred. If she isn't assisted in merging with the spirit of the old wise one that appears in her dream, she might suffer a psychotic breakdown and further behavioural disorders as the result of the fact that two obviously irreconcilable spirits have merged in one spectrum.'

'Vumani Bo?' Mama chants, asking if we agree with the divination.

'Siyavuma!' We all concur in a chorus.

'Vumani Bo?'

'Siyavuma!'

Mama clears her throat and makes grunting sounds. She whips the air with her cow-tail whisk. She hovers her nostrils above the burning impepho and says, 'Ignorance to the emergence of the ancestral spirit will create problems for your daughter and your family. The existence of the psychic phenomena cannot be thwarted forever as those from beyond will have the final say.' Mama delivers the message of caution.

'The ancestral spirit sees something striking and significant in your daughter, and thus trusts her ability to fulfil the calling. The old wise ones are drawn to those who have more awareness outside the physical focus and are not completely desensitised. Their sensitivity can be viewed as a precursor for the calling.'

'Can we plead with the ancestors to let my child be and lead a normal life?' asks the mother of the child with anguish in her popping eyes.

'As I said earlier, the messages cannot be ignored forever, the ancestral spirit might attempt to get the attention of other members of the family until someone responds to the call wholeheartedly. The bombardment of messages from beyond will be sustained until your daughter listens and if she continues to refuse, she will become unstable. The best cure is to say "yes" to the calling unreservedly. Once an ancestral spirit has identified someone to fulfil a purpose, the individual can run but cannot hide from the all-seeing of old.' Mama shares the naked truth.

'What needs to be done, Makhosi?' the mother of the child asks with a heavy voice.

'Traditional ceremonies need to be done to aid her in this calling. The rituals will open a relationship between her and the ancestors and reveal deeper messages contained by those of old. We'll have to do an initiation ceremony for her to legitimately honour the calling. She will then become a thwasa and observe the strict code of conduct in her journey to transcend the world of form into the world of the spirits. My role is to merge the spirit of your daughter with old wise ones and discover the identity of the spirit that's holding her absolute attention and wanting to be born again through her.'

The woman nods her head in agreement.

'Spirits usually associate with the natural kingdom, especially the ocean, rivers, mountains, caves or forests and, in your daughter's case, the ancestral spirit visits her in the guise of the spirit of Mthonyama River. She will be drawn to other natural splendours and find healing and calmness as a result.' Mama reveals the truth in the meaning.

'It will be necessary to go to the Mthonyama River to do a ritual ceremony there in order to merge your daughter's spirit with the spirit of the river to gain the power needed for development to higher planes. The spirit of the old wise one who is in the guise of the river will give guidance as to how to best fulfil the spiritual quest. We will slaughter a chicken as a sacrifice, baptise your daughter in the river, and ask the high spirits to journey with us on this road less travelled.' Mama paints the road ahead.

'It is my duty to assist your daughter to reconcile the energies of both worlds to enable her to serve as a bridge between the two realities and become a sangoma; healing the many across the land with knowledge gained from time immemorial.'

'Vumani Bo?'

'Siyavuma!'

The mother of the child swallows hard and takes a deep breath; she looks at Mama with unknowing eyes and says,

'I will relay all that you have told me to the elders of the family. I don't think there'll be an obstacle in allowing her to be initiated; but what I do need clarity on is what you will need from the family to do the initiation ceremony?' the mother asks.

'In order for me to start the healing process, you will have to appease the ancestors with a goat and that will be a symbol of the working relationship and connection between our ancestors. You will also need to bring three cocks for the ceremony; one should be red-feathered, one white and one grey. We will also need candles for the evening ceremony and maize to make fermented sorghum beer.' Mama lists the priorities to aid the initiation.

'You will have to also bring samp and beans to cook umngqusho to feed those in attendance and finely ground maize for porridge. The head of your clan and elders must come to bestow blessings on your daughter as she takes the passage to those that have gone long before her. It is also important to be sensitive to the higher spirit guides and listen to their intentions as they are taking the lead in this journey.' Mama imparts another pearl of wisdom.

'There are a few rituals and ceremonies to be observed at different stages of this journey but I will have to limit what I say to you so as not to confuse you. That's all I will tell you for now; relay your experience here to the members of your family and the spirits will guide you on what to do next.'

'Camagu.' The woman expresses her gratitude.

'Chosi,' Mama responds in acknowledgement.

The woman and her daughter leave the homestead with an air of wonder and resignation to the unknown.

Fourteen

It's been an unusual day indeed. The sun rose hesitantly from behind the distant mountains. The morning has been uninspiring. Even the birds didn't sing lively tunes to welcome the new day. The wind is sluggish and humid. There's reserved grief that is lingering. News of Nomkhubulwana's 'death' has spread. She was an unconventional woman to many but all knew the wisdom she possessed and she was respected the land over.

The confidence in my stride is suspended; there's a big lump in my throat that refuses to go. Nomkhubulwana's passing to the land beyond reminds me yet again that we are visitors here; our mission in the land of the walking dead comes to an end at some point. Life is a cycle of existence, we are born to die and we die to be born again, yet my heart is heavy with grief that knows no end. Nomkhubulwana's departure among us mere mortals seems sudden.

'One of these mornings I'll be gone.' Her premonition rings loud and true.

She taught me so much and shared all her wisdom about the book of life; love is what I have for her. To some extent, I am because of her; she fuelled the spiritual force within that gave me wings to realise more of my self. She is my other half; I love her like I love me. We shared dreams and we travelled together to different worlds. I bathed in her wisdom and learnt a lot from her; oh such light that shone so bright.

My heart feels heavy with emotions never aroused. How can the one so young at heart leave us so soon? The stage seemed to be set for her to breathe new life into our everyday existence. She possessed so much love. We danced in conversation for hours on end and I was a slave to her rhythm. She exuded royalty. She blessed me with her wisdom. I felt her essence and she took me on a journey to a deeper inner self. She unravelled the different rivers and streams that proceed to the ocean of love. She told me stories never told; stories the ancient wise chose to hide in parables and abstract proverbs.

Some people come into our lives and they go; some stay for a while and we are never quite the same. She represents the latter to me. She paved the way; her bright light narrated ancient stories and her overwhelming love melted hearts. There is so much work that she did in the hidden recesses of people's awareness; I wish the people of the land could've got to know her and appreciate the work she did. I miss her.

I saw her in my dreams before we met in person. I was perplexed when I saw her in the flesh; my mind kept saying, 'This is the person I saw in my dream.'

It was like I knew her in a different lifetime. I couldn't talk to her properly on that first encounter. I was rattled. I had goosebumps. Her light was too bright.

She paved the way and fulfilled her purpose. She showed me glimpses of the future when I was searching, full of anxiety and so unsure. She is a goddess; her smiling eyes told stories of innocence and she oozed the universal unified ancestral energy. I felt so at home in her presence. There was much strength in her stride as she strolled with a gait that revealed the convictions of her heart.

My story is her story and her story is my story. We share the same message. We are the children of the star in service of the high one. We are cut from the same cloth. All hail Nomkhubulwana.

All hail starlight. You will forever be in my heart of hearts.

Daydreams visit as I sit alone in the hut. I see Nomkhubulwana in the hidden corridors of my dreams. She smiles and waves. She sprinkles good fortune my way.

'We are the chosen ones,' she whispers from beyond the rainbow of dreams. 'It's all going to be okay,' she assures me. 'Remove the malady of self-doubt and move forth with conviction.' She lets me in on one of the secrets of life. 'Ubabalwe.'

I see the contagious smile that she brandished at will. There's a part of me that wishes she was still here physically so I could witness her move mountains, but in the same breath, and when I get over my narrow-mindedness, I know she is moving wheels of manifestation in the afterlife. She's my heroine. She reflected pure love back at me. I will forever be grateful. I keep her in my heart and carry her spirit with every step forward. There is no doubt that she is an angel. I feel that our journey is yet to fulfil its ultimate purpose; so the journey continues.

I'm brought back from the world of dreams by someone calling my name.

'Nwelezelanga!' a voice shouts from outside.

I make my way out of the hut to investigate. I see some of the herdboys taking their livestock to the hills.

'Let's go,' says Mongi, one of the herdboys.

I take the cows out of the kraal and join the boys. We make our way towards the Vezinyawo forest. We take the cows to the Muntu-Muntu lake for a drink. The harsh sun gives the boys a good reason to swim. I remain on the banks of the lake and make life forms out of clay. A silly raucous laughter echoes as the boys splash in the water and chase each other. Many lessons that come with age are revealed in these moments of play. The spirit of children is the most wild and agile; the unknown fascinates us.

I marvel at the world of ants as the boys busy themselves with stick-fighting. Dambuza calls me to come and watch but I shrug off the invitation. I kneel next to an anthill and observe the ants at work. I watch an army struggle to get a dead spider inside the opening of the anthill but reinforcement soon arrives to aid the work at hand. Another army goes out for the hunt and they seem to carry the same vision. The ants can teach us greatly about the march of civilisations; their rhythm beats with the rhythm of earth's heartbeat. They tell stories that have endured the passage of time. Their ways move like the ocean and align to the consciousness of the earth. They work with such zeal for the betterment of their community and plan for seasons yet to come. We miss the chance of humbling ourselves to the conquering kingdom of old. There's much more we can learn from the enlightened ones. The bees, the birds and the crabs hold divine messages for our evolutionary leap. The walking dead ignore the knowledge of yore that reveals that the current paradigm is destructive. The natural kingdom speaks profoundly and begs for our absolute attention at this hour.

These are the days to realise more of self.

Fifteen

MANY SEEKERS VISIT our homestead for different reasons. Some come to clear imbalances in their aura so that good fortune may come their way. A large number come to have their confusing dreams interpreted. Many have visited our household seeking relief for their physical ailments and there are those who come seeking advice on how to bring back a straying spouse. There are countless reasons that drive the many to come and see Mama for consultation. There are many who come without knowing the reason they are drawn to our homestead; Mama lets them stay until such time that the reason is revealed.

'Vuka, Nwelezelanga,' Mama wakes me up from a deep slumber.

'The sun is standing tall and you're still sleeping!' she reprimands. 'A girl should be awake before sunrise.' She gives me a tongue-lashing.

'I couldn't wake up, Mama; I had a recurring dream that arrested me in the world of the spirits.' I convey the reason for my having overslept.

'There was this woman ...'

'Light impepho before you say anything further,' Mama interjects.

I light the dry everlasting plant and it gives off a spicy smell.

'Go on. What did this woman do?' Mama asks with mild concern written on her forehead.

'She was weeping on top of a mountain. I felt her pain and brokenness. She seemed to be reaching out for me somehow. She was calling on me with her heart of hearts. I felt so drawn to her and she felt like a part of me. I wanted to wake up but she wasn't letting go and held on to my attention tightly.'

Mama takes a pouch containing animal bones, seashells, pieces of ivory, crocodile teeth, crystals, pieces of different metals and other interesting objects and blows into the pouch and tells me to do the same. She shakes the pouch and then throws its contents on the reed mat. She observes the revelations from the positioning of the items. She takes her charmed cow-tail whisk lying next to her and begins whipping the air, driving away unwanted spirits.

'Vumani bo?' she exclaims.

'Siyavuma,' I concur.

'I see a woman on a mountain summit; she is reaching out for you, my child.' Mama decodes the message.

'Who is she?' I enquire.

'Silence; listen!' Mama scolds me. 'She seems suicidal and desperate to see you,' she carries on. 'There's a deep connection she has with you; this woman gave birth to you, my child.' Mama reveals the hidden truth.

An odd feeling engulfs me. The revelation evokes deep emotions that were suppressed for the longest time. I grew up with Mama telling me that I was a blessed child who came with the rain. She always said that the Mflolozi River gave birth to me and that I was the luckiest child to have three mothers. I've never really thought much about my biological mother though. She's no different to me than the characters in folk tales. She was a figment of my imagination and I never really invested much feeling in her existence. Yet, I always had a slight curiosity though to see her someday.

'Will I ever see her, Mama?' I enquire.

'I don't know my child; I really don't know.' Mama conveys her uncertainty.

Aunt Nontsebenzo enters with dishes of porridge.

'Yhu, kufuneka usinde apha, Nwelezelanga,' Aunt Nontsebenzo instructs that I should coat the floor with cow dung.

'Ndizokwenza njalo, Aunty,' I oblige as instructed.

We eat the porridge in awkward silence. The new revelations evoke feelings I cannot describe.

'Where is Zimasa?' Mama breaks the ice.

'She is watering the vegetable garden,' Aunt Nontsebenzo responds.

'Tell her to come and eat, Nwelezelanga,' Mama orders.

I dash outside to call Zimasa.

'Zimasa, Mama is asking for you.'

She joins us a moment later.

Mama tells Aunt Nontsebenzo about the dream I had and what it means. The dog barks outside furiously as Mama unravels the deeper meaning of my dream.

'That dog is such a menace; quickly check why it is barking,' Mama asks.

I oblige as requested; I see it barking at our visitor. I whistle and call the dog.

'Mabhulu, Mabhulu! Come here.'

Mabhulu comes to me, wagging his tail, and jumps at me.

'You are naughty, wena,' I say to him.

'Hehe, this dog doesn't know me all of sudden,' says our neighbour Ma Ntuli.

'He is just naughty this one,' I respond.

'Naughty? This bloody dog almost bit me and you say it's just "naughty!"' Ma Ntuli scolds me.

'Uxolo Ma.' I excuse Mabhulu's behaviour.

'Is your mother in?' she asks.

'Yes, Ma, she is in the big hut.'

Ma Ntuli proceeds to the big hut. Curiosity gets the better of me and I follow her to listen to the reason for her visit this early in the morning. Ma Ntuli knocks at the door.

'Come in,' Aunt Nontsebenzo responds.

'Molweni,' Ma Ntuli greets those inside.

'Eweke,' Mama obliges to the greeting.

'Yhiyo, please forgive me for visiting this early in the morning but I had to come and tell you of the painful and disgusting news I have just heard,' says Ma Ntuli with a dramatic expression.

'Yintoni ngoku makhelwane!' Mama digs for details.

'The news is spreading like wildfire my neighbour; the corpse of a little girl was found in the forest.'

'Uthini ngoku makhelwane!' Mama expresses her shock upon hearing the news.

'The corpse was cut open with the insides exposed and the genitals missing.' Revulsion is written all over Ma Ntuli's face.

'The body was mutilated and her eyes gouged out.'

My stomach turns on hearing these details.

'Yoh, yoh, yoh, these witches are finishing our children,' Mama exclaims.

'Who is the girl?' asks Aunt Nontsebenzo curiously.

'It's that young sparkling girl with albinism from the Madiba clan in Dwesi village,' Ma Ntuli tells us.

'Black magic is spreading like a plague,' says Mama defeatedly.

'Say that again, makhelwane.' Ma Ntuli shares in the sentiment.

'I'm told that the chief visited the family and consoled them. The royal house will investigate the matter and hopefully the culprit will be apprehended and stoned to death. There will be an imbizo at the royal house tomorrow morning to talk about the scourge that has infested our land.' Ma Ntuli informs us of the meeting.

'You see Zimasa and Nwelezelanga why I always tell you not to wander in the forest alone; you must always go in groups, even when you go to pick up wood,' Mama reiterates.

'Our children are persecuted, murdered and mutilated for greed and evil intentions,' Ma Ntuli carries on.

'How long are we going to let this terror reign, huh?' Mama asks with a defeated voice.

I shiver as fear creeps in under my skin. I imagine the horror the victims must have experienced. It must have been awful being pounced on by these barbarians and dragged to the nearest bush to be slaughtered. The hair on my body stands up.

'Remember that child with albinism from Khanyayo village that was kidnapped two moons ago?' Aunt Nontsebenzo chips in.

'The poor child was abducted from her home as she slept in the hut with her siblings. She was found in a nearby bush dismembered. These witches have no shame. Her eyes were also gouged out, her ears were missing and her private part was cut off.'

The details of these atrocities make me squeamish.

'Why are they doing this to our children?' asks Ma Ntuli dismayed.

'Children with albinism are the most prized as their innocence is highly valued,' Mama responds.

'This is sickening,' says Ma Ntuli, with loathing written all over her face.

'These witches stoop so low because of greed and the perceived wealth gain from these wicked acts,' says Aunt Nontsebenzo.

'There was another incident I heard of some time ago in Mkhambathi village where the corpse of a person with albinism was disinterred and then stolen. The family had only buried the deceased the day before.' Mama tells us of another evil deed.

'That heinous act definitely disturbed the peace of the deceased,' Ma Ntuli adds.

'It is hard for our children to roam freely. They live in

fear and are treated as outcasts by the villagers and are ostracised. It is really shameful.' Mama makes another passionate observation.

'Eish, now you've got me going! My heart is racing! I was informed of another terrible tragedy where a stepfather sold his stepdaughter. He was involved in the planning of her abduction and chopped off her arms but she lived to tell the tale.' Mama fills us in on yet another gory act.

'The incident left her traumatised and she was never quite the same. She is mentally disturbed and has never got over the ordeal,' Mama carries on.

'Yoh, our children are hunted like animals.' Ma Ntuli throws her hands up in the air.

'There is an active cabal of witches who peddle and perpetuate dark spirits in our land. They sacrifice children with albinism to appease dark lords.' Mama conveys the ugly fact.

'Our children are killed and maimed for the purpose of those who believe that they will gain power and success as a result of taking a mixture of medicine made from human parts,' Aunt Nontsebenzo reiterates. 'Children with albinism are raped in the hope of curing sexually transmitted diseases and for other obscure healing purposes,' she carries on.

'Families are motivated to kill their children with albinism at birth to avoid the stigma.' Mama serves another dose of the crazy reality.

We all sit in the hut filled with astonishment. The jaw-dropping wicked realities leave me dismayed. We are prey to these witches. Icy worms of apprehension crawl up my spine. I feel sick to my stomach. It is a bizarre kind of fear. I can't wrap my head around what these evil people are capable of. I think again of the terror the victims must have felt when their fate met these dark forces. The truth leaves me breathless and knocks the wind out of me.

Shame on you, barbarians. Shame on you evil souls of forever-night.

Sixteen

THE SUN RISES AS the cock crows welcome the lord of day. The morning is somehow uncharacteristically cold for this time of the year. We sit in the main hut; Zimasa is making a fire to boil water for Mama's cup of tea. She puts the enamel teapot on the fire. The burning impepho circulates in the hut, evoking calm to all those inside it. Mama relays a dream she had at nightfall.

'Yoh, I had a curious dream, Nontsebenzo,' Mama says.

'What was the dream about, sisi?' Aunty asks inquisitively.

'Eish, there was a meeting of the old wise ones in the kraal. They sat in a circle on wooden benches, passionately discussing issues concerning the clan,' Mama narrates with a little unease in her voice.

'They talked for hours and hours until the rising sun was high at noon. One of the elders called me and asked me to fill the empty calabash with the traditional brew. I went looking for the sorghum beer but the containers were dry and empty; I looked in all the huts but there was none to be found. They kept sending children to ask why I was taking so long as they were thirsty.' Mama still carries the anxiety in her heart.

'It was clear that there was no traditional beer in the homestead. I was so anxious and my heart was beating faster and faster not knowing what to do. I spent the rest of the dream in a complete panic looking for something that I knew was not there.' She breathes heavily.

'I woke up very early this morning still feeling troubled. The elders are thirsty, Nontsebenzo. I have to make the traditional brew for them and invite the members of our clan to honour the occasion,' she says to Aunty.

'Yoh sisi, we have to get on it, we don't want to make the old wise ones angry,' says Aunt Nontsebenzo, a little shaken.

'You don't have to remind me, Nontsebenzo, I know the wrath of the old when their peace is disturbed.' Mama emphasises the point.

Zimasa offers Mama a cup of tea and places a small three-legged cast-iron pot on the fire to boil water for the porridge.

'Girls, you'll have to go to the forest to collect wood later,' Mama says gently.

'Okay, Mama,' Zimasa and I respond in a chorus.

'Let's go and fetch water, Nwelezelanga, and fill up the tank,' says Aunt Nontsebenzo.

I fetch two buckets from the middle hut and give one to Aunt Nontsebenzo. She leads the way to the nearby stream. We scoop the water into the buckets and make our way back to the homestead. Aunt Nontsebenzo leads the way once again with the bucket of water on top of her head and both her hands placed on her waist; walking with the gait of a seductive goddess.

I collect cow dung from the kraal on my return and coat the floor of the big hut. Zimasa waters the vegetable garden in front of the semicircle of huts. Aunt Nontsebenzo goes to the stream for another refill. Mama grinds corn on a stone in preparation for the traditional brew. We work to stay alive and keep up with the earth's heartbeat.

'Nwelezelanga! Let's go and collect wood!' Zimasa shouts to me from outside the hut.

'Uyiphethe inkatha?' I remind Zimasa not to forget to take a cloth to cushion her head from the wood.

'Yes, I've got one,' she confirms.

We make our way out of the homestead. Mabhulu wags his tail as he gallops ahead of us. Zimasa sings her favourite song. I join her in the chorus and back her as we cross the nearby stream. We chase the playful butterflies along the way.

'Nomtha!' Zimasa calls her friend as we approach her homestead.

'Nomtha!' she shouts again.

Nomtha steps outside the hut to answer the call.

'Masiyotheza!'

'I will meet you on top of the hill,' Nomtha replies.

We carry on walking towards the top of the hill, singing in the open fields. There is freedom in the air and a lightness in our mood. We skip and dance our way up the hill. We search for mushrooms as we wait for Nomtha at the top. She comes a moment later carrying a machete to cut the wood; she is singing a melodious tune as she approaches us. Zimasa picks a mushroom and shows off her find.

'Look, it's so big,' she gloats to make me jealous. 'Where's yours?' she adds insult to injury by rubbing in the fact that I haven't found one.

'Did you have to bring her?' Nomtha asks Zimasa in displeasure.

'Don't start now Nomtha; leave her alone,' Zimasa says in my defense.

'She must go and herd the cattle with the boys.' Nomtha rolls her eyes. 'Zimasa, we can't go with her; she is a big gossiper this one. She tells the boys our private conversations,' Nomtha protests.

'Leave her alone; there's literally no wood at home; we need the extra hands,' Zimasa insists.

We make our way into the forest. There is always a festive mood when we go to the forest. It's as if it's a celebration of the loosening grip of the hands of the grown-ups who dictate the terms at home. We pick wild berries and other wild fruit along the way. Zimasa suddenly sprints ahead to pick another mushroom before any of us notice it. She gloats yet again.

'You're not getting any,' she says to me, proud of her find.

The conversation quickly changes to the favourite topic Zimasa and Nomtha seem to like more than any other when they are away from the ears of our mothers; they go on and on about the cutest boys in the village.

'My friend, who's more handsome between Qhawe and Mpondo?' Nomtha asks Zimasa.

'It's Qhawe, my friend, without a shadow of a doubt,' Zimasa readily answers with excitement.

'I don't know what you like about that ugly swine with a big forehead,' Nomtha shoots back. 'Mpondo is the one; he's got royal blood.' She points out her favourite.

'Pleeeease, you should tell him to wash his armpits; he stinks like a rotten cabbage,' says Zimasa with disapproval written all over her face.

'Jealousy doesn't suit you, my friend,' says Nomtha.

'What do you think, Nwelezelanga?' Zimasa asks for my opinion.

'We don't need her lousy input, she's a boy; this one will die alone.' Nomtha taunts me as always.

We look for dry bushes to cut wood and I soon spot a fallen tree.

'There's a tree we can cut,' I say to the girls.

Nomtha takes the lead and cuts off the branches of the tree with the machete. Zimasa and I look for dry bush in the surrounding area. We find some and start breaking off pieces and putting them in a pile. While we're busy with the task, I hear a curious bird call.

'Did you hear that?' I ask Zimasa.

She ignores me and carries on collecting wood. The singing echoes behind the myriad forest sounds. It is both beautiful and mesmerising in an unearthly manner. The call seduces me like a moth to a flame. It stops for a moment and other forest sounds appear after being overshadowed by the mysterious bird call. Before I can digest what is happening the bird sings a harmony that penetrates the heart and fills it with awe. I follow the melody with caution and hesitation in my stride. Curiosity leads the way. The magical adventure wakes every fibre of my body. I walk down a winding footpath, moving in the general direction of the sound. The sun dances and sparkles as the wind caresses the vegetation. I stray away from the path into the untamed territory of the forest. The singing calls in a definite voice. I reach an opening in the growth and it leads me to a patch of land with no grass. I see a curious circle of lit candles on the floor of the forest. The flames of the candles dance with the wind in a magical exhibition. There are crystals placed in the middle of the circle. Awe and fascination fill my heart. A man with a white robe appears from nowhere. He has defined facial features. The small eyes, the square forehead, dark lips and somewhat pointy nose make him alluring. There's a calming presence about him.

'I see you, Nwelezelanga.' The voice quenches my thirsty heart.

I stand still, entranced by the moment.

'Sit down, my child,' the man says with caring authority.

He gestures with his hand that I should sit in the middle of the circle. I sit in the centre surrounded by the burning candles and I feel a surge of lightness in my being. He sits down at the north side. He begins to tell me a folk tale about the beginning of time; his voice transfixes me, it is both fantastic and alien. I hear him but I somehow can't digest the meaning of the words. It is like listening to a song and not understanding the words. As I look into his eyes, I feel drawn to him somehow; he hypnotises me into the depths of his soul. He continues to speak in this beautiful language I don't understand. He steals my essence. I'm paralysed by the effect of his spell. There are stories across the land of children who are stolen and turned into zombies to be playthings for their masters. He offers me a 'magic potion' that he says will give me everlasting youth and I drink it without question. The potion renders me motionless and I feel sick. I collapse to the floor and my body begins to seize. My stomach churns in pain. I feel the strength ebbing out of my body. I progress to a vegetative state. I see the luminous bright light coming from the world beyond. The phosphorescent-like glow draws me. I get glimpses of the land of origins; the children of the star call with a definite voice and ask me to let go and free myself from all the earthly heartaches. They beg me to embrace the gift of death and join them in the playground of eternity. A part of me misses the freedom and carefree nature of being completely spirit. The man addresses me in his authoritative voice.

'You are mine. You are my zombie. Your soul is my plaything and I can will it to do whatever I want,' he roars with surety in his voice.

'Hahaha, you thought you were invincible. They say you are the special one, look at you now,' he scorns.

'Hahaha.' His evil laugh echoes through the forest.

I lie suspended on the forest floor paralysed, unable to move but very much conscious and sane.

'I am the true diviner and prophet of the land. You thought I'd sit and watch while you stole my shine?' he shouts. The killer instinct glistens in his eyes.

I don't understand what the man is saying; he mumbles uncontrollably for a while.

Suddenly Mabhulu appears and barks at the man, sensing his evil intentions. Zimasa and Nomtha call my name. The man is startled and quickly slips away into the bushes. The girls arrive at the scene; Zimasa wails upon seeing me.

'Yhuuuu, child of my mother! What have they done to you!' she cries and shakes me violently.

'Nwelezelanga!' she shouts my name with deep distress in her voice.

'Nwelezelanga!' she shakes me yet again, begging for my response.

I wish I could respond and release the pain in her heart. I look at her without expressing any emotion. I am no different to a statue. Zimasa puts me on her back and starts walking home.

Seventeen

Mama feeds me awful-tasting concoctions every few hours while I lie on the reed mat. There's a saying among traditional healers that a serious malady is cured with a bitter medicine, and I can testify to that. The air that circulates the hut is humid, stale and sickening. There is little cool air coming in through the wide-open door and windows as the sun beats down outside. I feel hot and uncomfortable. There's a damp cloth on my forehead to keep my temperature down. Mama parries away the flies on my face with a cloth.

Anxiety is thick in the air as Mama tries to remedy the situation. Aunt Nontsebenzo and Zimasa help where they can. The mood is hijacked by the depressing atmosphere. Mama feeds me yet another concoction of medicine in her attempt to bring me back to the apparent reality. The paralysis renders me motionless. Beads of sweat stream down my face. Mama takes the cloth that's on my forehead, dips it in water, squeezes it out and wipes away the sweat on my face and neck. She rinses the cloth yet again, squeezes it out, folds the cloth into a square and puts it back on my forehead.

The sombre mood continues to suffocate and Mama lights some impepho to chase away the dense and unwanted energies that circulate. She mumbles low under her breath.

She increases the volume of her voice and begs with passion for the all-knowing one to put a healing hand over me.

'Oh Mvelinqangi, the great Nkulunkulu, I bow to your might. Oh Thongo lam, knowing ones of old, please hear me. Please remove the shadow of death hanging over my precious daughter,' she prays. 'Please breathe strength into her joints and will her to stand on her feet. Let this medicine heal her to her old self,' she pleads.

Mama takes the impepho and circles the room while praying for a 'miracle'. She snorts and speaks in twisted tongues. She comes closer to me and hovers the burning everlasting plant close to my nostrils.

'Get well my child,' she whispers. 'Oh Nkwenkwezi, my dearest child, wake up.'

She looks at me with endearing and rheumy eyes; tears break and fall down her cheeks. Zimasa enters with a bowl of porridge in her hand.

'It's still hot,' she tells Mama.

'Put it on top of the table for it to cool down a bit, my child,' says Mama. 'Is there warm water by the fire?' Mama asks Zimasa.

'There is hot water that I was going to use to make tea and wash the dishes,' responds Zimasa.

'Bring it my child; I want to wash your sister before she eats.'

Zimasa steps outside to the middle hut and brings the hot water inside.

'The washbasin is under the table,' Mama tells Zimasa upon her return.

Zimasa puts the small three-legged cast-iron pot on the floor and takes the washbasin from underneath the table. She pours the water.

'Please clip a few leaves of lavender for me, my child.'

Zimasa goes outside to clip the leaves from the lavender plant next to the entrance of the homestead. Mama puts the washbasin down next to me. Zimasa comes back with the lavender leaves and Mama takes some of the leaves and places them inside my pillow. She then puts some in the hot water. She rubs the lavender leaves in her hands and hovers her scented hands close to my nose. The smell evokes a feeling of calm and I'm lost in the heavens of the heart for a moment. Mama adds a bit of cold water to the washbasin to make the water mild and ready for my bath. She lifts me up and makes me sit against the wall and then takes off my kanga. She dips the cloth in the water and washes my face and neck. She lifts my arms and washes my armpits. She breathes heavily as a result of the physical exertion. Beads of sweat form in her nose and on her forehead. She washes my chest, breast and belly. She struggles when turning me around to wash my back. I feel sorry for her and I feel like a nuisance for putting her through this hardship. She washes me from the waist down and then takes the washbasin and throws the dirty water on a patch of grass outside.

I feel refreshed and light in body, as if layers of oppressive energy have been lifted. The heavy burden on Mama is evident for all to see. She presents a strong demeanour to all so no one loses hope, and it's admirable, but I cannot escape the guilt that haunts me for the burden I've caused.

'Please bring me that porridge, Zimasa,' she asks.

Zimasa obliges as instructed and Mama feeds me the almost-cold porridge. She is patient with me as I take long to swallow. She wipes my mouth thereafter.

I become weaker and weaker. My temperature drops. I feel cold and start to shiver. My teeth chatter. Mama covers my body with a blanket. Worry chokes me. I will myself to wake up but the effort is in vain. I summon strength yet again but the status quo remains. Mama feeds me another revolting medicine that shocks my taste buds. A surge of burning energy sweeps through my body. I suddenly feel hot and begin to sweat. Mama wipes the beads of sweat and removes the blanket. I vomit the porridge I ate earlier. I choke and cough violently.

'My child!' exclaims Mama.

She lifts me and props me up against the wall. I continue to cough violently. She pats my back repeatedly.

'Phuma Mthakathi.' She calls upon the evil spirits to leave me.

She holds my head with both hands and swings it in all directions to shake off the spirits that have possessed me.

'Get out you spirit of darkness. Go away you evil spirit. Disappear to the trenches of forever-night.'

She pours me a glass of water and holds the back of my head. with her left hand and makes me drink the water slowly. I try to drink but most of it spills down the sides of my mouth.

'Zimasa, please bring me that reed mat and that blanket.'

Mama wipes my mouth and moves me on top of the clean blanket that Zimasa has brought. Mama takes the soiled blanket and mat outside and comes back with warm water which she pours into the washbasin. She washes my upper body to get rid of the stench of vomit that lingers. She then smears my body with scented oil and wraps me in a clean kanga. She gives me another cocktail of medicine in order to clean my stomach and release the waste in my bowels. Aunt Nontsebenzo enters the hut.

'Do you need help, sisi?' Aunt Nontsebenzo asks kindly.

'Please take the dirty blankets and wash them in the river,' says Mama, 'and ask Zimasa to cook sweet potatoes for Nwelezelanga,' Mama asks Aunt Nontsebenzo as she's about to step out of the door.

Mama piggybacks me to the long-drop toilet. I am introduced to a new level of love that knows no end; a love I never knew existed. Mama still carries a lot of pride in this seemingly hopeless situation. She puts me on the toilet. My stomach growls; the medicine has worked and my stomach is loose. I flush the waste in my bowels down the long drop. Mama grinds her teeth and cringes as she wipes my behind. Tears fall down my face from the humiliation of it all. Mama piggybacks me back to the main hut. She lays me on top of the blanket.

Another day passes as evening falls in the rural heartland of Dingilizwe. Life has become a drag in our household. Zimasa serves samp and beans to Aunt Nontsebenzo and Mama. She brings me mashed sweet potatoes.

'Thank you, my child,' Mama offers gratitude to my older sister.

Mama feeds me before she eats. Everyone is quiet and the buzzing mosquitoes fill the silence. The sound of the spoon touching the plate tells the story of our lives. The mood is gloomy and uninspiring. Mama eats her food once she finishes feeding me. Zimasa stands up to put her plate on the table.

'Here Zimasa, take my plate,' says Aunt Nontsebenzo.

She takes the plate from Aunt Nontsebenzo and places both the plates on top of each other on the small table in the north end of the room. She then goes out to the middle hut and comes back with a bucket of water and puts it on top of the table. She scoops out some water with a cup and drinks in one long gulp.

'Can I also have some, my child?' Mama asks.

Zimasa brings Mama a cup of water.

'Thank you, my angel, please put it here.' Mama points next to her.

'Your eyes look reddish, you must be tired.' Mama shares her observation.

'I am, Mama,' responds Zimasa as she walks sluggishly to the bed.

She climbs into bed, tucks herself under the covers and falls asleep; Aunt Nontsebenzo follows soon thereafter. Mama burns the leaves of a dry sage plant. She then fiddles around looking for something at her altar. She finds the candle she was looking for, lights it and brings it to my side. She also has a tiny razor and a small bottle of powdered medicine at hand. She goes back to her altar and finds some liquid medicine. She gives me three spoons of the unpleasant-tasting remedy. She unwraps my kanga and makes tiny razor incisions all over my body, with emphasis on the joints. She then rubs the powdered medicine in the cuts.

'Phila mntan'am,' she whispers under her breath.

A tingling sensation circulates under my skin. Mama wraps me with the kanga once again and covers me with a blanket.

'Sleep well, my dear child.'

Mama prepares to sleep. She drinks the glass of water next to her and blows out the candle and rests. I lie awake in the dark. I want to let go and release myself from this burden. I oscillate between wakefulness and the world of dreams. I see the beautiful ones of yore and they smile and giggle, calling me to come and play with them. The children of the star beg me to answer their call. They don't understand my attachment to the land of the walking dead. They lure me to the world of spirits but I still have links to this world.

My biological mother suddenly appears in my dreams. She is full of suicidal thoughts but at the same time has a great yearning to see me. I want to release her from the self-inflicted pain so she can find peace in her heart. I'm caught in these different worlds. I want to let go and be swallowed by the highways of eternity but intuition tells me to connect with my biological mother and release her from the pain she carries with her. I pray for strength and a miracle.

'Oh Somandla, I humble myself to you. Please help me regain my strength. Relieve me from this nightmare, oh great Nkulunkulu. You are the lord of miracles and I ask for one this very moment. Give vigour to my joints and breathe your spirit of power in my entire body.'

I project my heart of hearts to the all-knowing one and receive all the blessings. I pray to Qamata asking for guidance. I ask the high one to fill my body with vitality so I can fulfil my last earthly wish. I believe in the magic of miracles; believing is reality and reality is existence. I pray for the healing hand of the almighty to sprinkle the magic of life back into me. I beg the nine gods of the nine heavens to come to my aid. The gates of eternity are flung open and the prayers are honoured.

Eighteen

DEATH KNOCKS AT THE door demanding to be let in; the gnawing knowledge that the end of the journey is nigh fills my heart with sadness. It is not the fear of death nor my clinging to the physical actuality that has bred apprehension in my mortal self but rather the emotional turmoil that I feel is sucking the very life from my biological mother's heart. The ominous feelings make her unsettled and unready to let go of past misdemeanours. My heart yearns to release her from the bondage of guilt and let her know that all is well in my soul and I forgave her before I was born.

I pray to the lord of lords deep in the ten gates of eternity with deep emotions. I summon the all-knowing Qamata to hear me. I appeal to the lesser gods of the nine heavens in the gateway of eternity to plead on my behalf. I pray to the high one to wake me up from the deep slumber. I ask for strength to go and search for my mother.

'Oh Mvelinqangi, the shining light in all the darkness; oh Sonini-nanini, knower of great truths from beyond; I humble myself to your might and wisdom, oh all-knowing one,' I plead passionately.

'Allow me to relieve the heavy load and burden my mother has had to carry ever since I was born, oh Somandla.'

I express the feelings deep within.

'Please hear me, great Nkulunkulu. Please fill my body with strength so I can look for her.' I request divine intervention.

'Show me where she is, oh almighty Qamata.' I bow in all humbleness.

We are presented with challenges in order to grow. Pain visits us when the trial is beyond our comprehension. The hidden wisdom is only revealed once we rise above the level of the paradox and therefore attain a higher state of self.

I reach for my mother in the faraway spheres of pure dreams, flowing with the impartial winds searching even the forbidden territories in the unknown world. I surf the tide of time to all of its seven corners and reach the clouds above and they reveal untold secrets that bring calm to my spirit. Forever and eternity stare in awe at my deep passion to see my mother and all is granted.

I see my mother; I feel her heavy heart and her hopelessness evokes tears in my soul. I see her ready to jump off the mighty cliff to her death. I shout out, 'Oh mother of my flesh and blood! Oh mother of my creation, through the passage of your womb into this world I came and your mission was fulfilled.' She melts my heart.

'You served your destiny in that respect and my heart will be forever filled with gratitude that knows no end. Oh daughter of the soil, I am reaching out to tell you that all is well. Do not invite death for what you think is an unfulfilled purpose. We were both given mysterious challenges to learn in life and to realise more of the self. The wise ones say that no soul remains forever ignorant and we should rise to that reality.'

The message travels far and wide and into her paining heart.

Tears ran down her face and hopelessness engulfed her spirit. She stood on the edge of the cliff ready to will death to her tortured self. Nokwakha saw no reason to live another day on the unforgiving earth. The seasons had long lost their fascination. All she wanted was to die and get away from the misery that followed her like a shadow. She looked up at the horizon and all she saw was a desert of lost hope. The natural kingdom depressed her. The birds made irritating sounds and the singing of crickets irked her profusely. She looked down the cliff and could see her dying moment playing out before her. A voice of reason whispered to her soul and said, 'Death will not bring you eternal resting peace.' The voice echoed in the deep corridors of her being.

'You may rest for a while after the perceived "death", however, you will have to face up to yourself and those abilities that you did not use.' Silence swallows the voice into the unmanifested.

She closed her eyes tightly, summoning all the courage to jump. She edged closer to her demise but the moment was interrupted by a deep and profound plea from an unknown voice. She heard it passionately begging her not to jump and the voice seemed to be echoing from the very mountain gorge. She didn't know if she was hallucinating but she was suddenly overwhelmed with fear and stepped back from the edge of the cliff. The pleading voice kept reverberating from deep within. She was mystified but the yearning to see the growth of the seed that was planted in her garden overwhelmed her. The changing winds whistled messages from the faraway lands; she trusted the unknown and obliged to the calling.

Water.

'Water,' I ask, to relieve my scratchy throat.

'My child!' Mama exclaims.

I wake up from my paralysis through the divine intervention of the all-knowing one. The almighty Qamata heeded my plea and granted me the chance to fulfil my heart's desire.

'My child!' Mama cries out again.

'Water.'

'Zimasa! Get some water! Quickly!'

Zimasa races out to the hut where meals are prepared and comes back with water. I gulp it down.

'All hail to you, oh all-knowing Qamata.' Mama gives due praises. 'We bow to you as these wretched mortals, oh Mvelinqangi.'

There is an air of relief circling the room. Mama and Aunt Nontsebenzo rejoice and ululate, thanking those of yore for obliging their prayers.

'How are you feeling, my child?' Mama enquires. 'Do you want some more water?'

'No thank you; I'm quenched, Mama,' I respond.

'How are you feeling Nkwenkwezi?' Mama asks yet again.

'I feel rested, Mama.'

'You have been in a deep sleep for quite some time, my child, and we were not sure when you would wake up from your "dream".' Mama fills me in on the episodes in the land of the walking dead.

Everyone looks at me with a touch of curiosity in their eyes. Aunt Nontsebenzo stares at me without saying a word; she seems flabbergasted by the turn of events. Zimasa keeps her distance and observes from the sidelines.

'Do you know how long you've been asleep, Nkwenkwezi?' Mama asks.

'I wasn't really asleep Mama; I was very much awake in my sleep.'

'What do you mean, my child?' Mama asks with deep interest.

'I travelled to different worlds, Mama. I saw future histories and listened to the stories of past.' I share my journey with her.

'I had a vision, Mama. I saw my biological mother and I recognised her instantly. She was full of anguish and is reaching out to me. She is yearning to see me; I have to meet her Mama.' I plead with heaviness in my voice.

'But you are not strong enough, Nwelezelanga.' Mama states the obvious with deep concern. 'And where are you going to meet her anyway?' She is perplexed by my intentions.

'The spirits tell me to go to the Mthonyama River. I have to trust that all will be revealed in due course. Time is not mine, Mama. I've been given this moment to fulfil the message from my dream. There are no certainties at all. I have to trust and honour my instinct. The wise ones usually say that there is knowing in the knowing that one doesn't know. I have to trust what can't be seen. I have to trust the feeling, Mama.'

Silence falls after my speech and speaks notorious riddles that turn the heart into knots.

Nineteen

I GO TO THE MYSTERIOUS Mthonyama River the following day. The day is one of glorious splendour and the birds sing songs of enchantment with enthusiasm. I float in and out of daydreams. I walk up and down the red hills of the land towards the Mojaji mountain. My heart pulsates with the rhythm of my stride. I pass grazing cows, goats and sheep. The sun beats unmercifully but it doesn't distract me from my quest. I reach the river at high noon. I sit on top of a big oval rock that rises above the lush vegetation under a big oak tree. The breeze strokes me gently as I sit under the all-watching heavens. The echo of the humming river travels with the wind and bathes the surrounds with mystical suggestions. The mood is perfect. Butterflies show off their purity and crickets chirp perfect melodies to the divine orchestra.

At first I thought I was high in a dream when I sensed the mood in the air change. While fluctuating between the world of form and daydreams, I hear a bristling sound in the long grass. My heart pounds as if it wants to burst out of my chest as I suspect a creature of the wild is on its way to attack me. I stand erect on top of the rock, anticipating the worst. I hold my knobkerrie high in my left hand but courage has long deserted me. I tremble with fear as the sound in the grass gets closer.

'Go away!' I shout.

The bristling movement continues my way.

'Go away you dragon of day.' I try to summon courage deep from the depths of my being but it seems so elusive.

The face of a woman appears. She looks at me with affectionate eyes full of warmth. Her watery eyes glaze as the sun basks the day, then tears fall from her round moon face. We're locked in each other's gaze and time seems to evaporate in that moment. A part of me knows her intimately and I was wandering beyond space and time to connect with the feeling. It is coming back to me with a sudden rush when she says, 'Is that you, my child?' The question bursts out of her.

'Mama,' I blurt out immediately as all connection to the woman in front of me is revealed.

She looks at me as if I am a lucky omen that has fallen from the blue heavens above. I burst into tears for all kingdoms to hear me and shower me with all their mercy. She looks at me and talks in silence, asking the riddles in her heart to be untangled. I jump off the rock and move towards her with a beaming smile on my face. She comes towards me with relief written all over her oval face. We fall into each other's embrace and I feel all the burdens lift off our shoulders and release us to a world of pure dreams.

'Forgive me my child for I have sinned; how can I justify my existence for what I did?' Guilt and excitement fill her heart. 'I deserve the harshest punishment for my evil deed.'

'I forgave Mama a long time ago. Let's not dwell on the past for the present is a gift.' I'm overwhelmed by her grace.

'I am grateful for this moment; glory to the all-knowing Qamata.' Mama sings praises to the divine one. 'The guilt exhausted me my child; I was swallowed into a rabbit hole. There was no more light in my days; a heavy dark cloud followed me everywhere I went and life exhausted me.' She opens her heart bare. 'I wished the earth would open up and swallow me so that the guilt could be forever buried deep in the belly of the ageless soil.'

Everything happens for a reason within the grand design of the natural splendour; we live and we learn and precious experience we earn.

We make our way back home holding hands. The conversation flows as we share our earthly existences. I tell her the story of my life and she shares the times of her hard living. I see a lot of me in her. We connect deeper in silence. I feel my strength waning and I become weaker with every step. The beating sun is making it worse. I don't express my discomfort to Mama. It is becoming evident that our reunion is actually our separation. Absolute truth reveals the beginning of the end; the end of this journey at least. My truth calls beyond the borders of this lifetime.

We reach the homestead and go into the big hut where everyone is sitting. Greetings are exchanged and I take the pleasure of introducing everyone to each other. Zimasa goes to make tea.

'Light impepho, Nwelezelanga,' says Mama as she sits on a reed mat next to her altar.

I stand up to take the impepho to the north end of the hut. I feel weak and dizzy; I faint and am plunged into the world of pure dreams.

Twenty

I SEE THE LIGHT. It is calling and calling. I've penetrated the halo. I'm becoming one with it. I'm slowly transforming; gearing for transcendence. Time is not mine. The ultimate god has already spoken and the lesser gods rejoice for the arrival of one of the children of the star. A sense of freedom and ecstasy fills my spirit as the life force drains out of my body. The purpose has been served. 'Death' is knocking, ready to transport me to higher planes. We die in order to grow in another reality. There is no point when the spirit vanishes. Life is a state of becoming and 'death' is part of the process of becoming. Both the form and the formless are states of aliveness but in varying degrees. My truth lies beyond the borders of this lifetime and the time to rise to that realisation has come.

The gateway to the land of origins has opened up. I'll have to journey through the blinding colourless light of emptiness to the land beyond. The children of the star wait at the gates of eternity, anticipating the return of one of their own. I leave behind heavy hearts. I wish I could dry the tears from their eyes. Absolute truth will eventually put their paining hearts at ease. Revelations will come articulating that the movement of time alchemises even the deepest suffering. My moment is nigh. The land of spirit calls with a definite voice; mine is to honour the command of the high one. My life flashes before my eyes in a moment that seems to last a lifetime of its own. I learn from all my immediate life events wholeheartedly. It's another opportunity for spiritual realisation; it is death of all illusion. My spirit reaches for the clouds in ascension to the realm of origins. Suddenly, I'm aware of all the truths that were concealed. The identification with time structures collapses and loses its fascination. I plant feelings of calm and understanding in all those I leave behind; the message is communicated in the deeper terrains of their subconscious. I summon all the strength to leave a message for their suffering hearts.

'Don't cry when I die as I will already be born again;
Celebrate, for there is birth within my death;
I came for a while and was rather pressed for time;
I came to love and to pass a message from beyond;
I promised not to stay a while longer;
I begged for more time in the distance yonder;
I flew too close to the sun and indulged in the exotic orgy of earthly desires;
Through the fires, I transcend, illuminate, giving birth to true self;
The circle continues bringing wonder to itself;
I want to fly really;
Cross the oceans with the birds of a feather;
Merge with the divine star and claim my worth in the land of origins;
And be reminded what it's like to be completely spirit.'

I slowly let go of the physical focus. Inside us lies a radiance, a most magnificent presence and it is this inner essence that we all justly desire and seek union with.

The last ounce of energy leaves the body; I'm gone already.

Okumhlophe kuwe.

Acknowledgements

There are many people who have sprinkled good fortune my way. There are those who were kind enough to be the bridge in order for this dream to be realised. I am grateful. I am humbled. Enkosi kakhulu, kakhulu. This journey has been a great teacher. I bow. Camagu!

About the Author

Unathi Magubeni is an Eastern Cape-based writer, sangoma and trainee herbalist, who left the corporate world in 2009. His first book, a collection of poetry called Food for Thought, was published in 2003. Nwelezelanga: The Star Child is his debut novel.

An Exciting New Look for BlackBird Books Fiction

This new BlackBird Books look is a result of a collaboration with Sindiso Khumalo, a textile designer based in London and Cape Town, who graciously designed the visuals for the series. Sindiso studied architecture at the University of Cape Town prior to moving to London, where she went on to study a Masters in Textiles at Central Saint Martins. Sindiso Khumalo founded her eponymous label with a focus on creating modern sustainable textiles with a strong emphasis on African storytelling. She designs the textiles in her collections by hand, using watercolours and collage. Over the years she has developed a uniquely colourful visual voice, which draws upon her Zulu and Ndebele heritage, and also speaks to the land of KwaZulu-Natal, where she is from. Sustainability, artistry and empowerment lie at the heart of the label.

In October 2015, Sindiso won Vogue Italia's "Who Is On Next?" competition in Dubai. Sindiso feels very passionate about fashion and empowerment. She has spoken at the United Nations on sustainability in fashion and is currently working closely with the UN ITC Ethical Fashion Initiative. She has presented her work at Milan Fashion Week with the mentorship of Camera Nazionale della Moda Italiana.

Her work has been exhibited at the Royal Festival Hall in London, the Smithsonian National Museum of African Art in Washington, the Louisiana Museum of Modern Art in Denmark and the Zeitz MOCAA in Cape Town. Her work has been published in Vogue Italia, Vogue UK, ELLE South Africa and Marie Claire South Africa as well as in the Louisiana Museum of Modern Art's "Africa: Architecture, Culture and Identity" collection. Her previous clients include IKEA, Woolworths South Africa and Vodacom.

Other BlackBird Books fiction titles

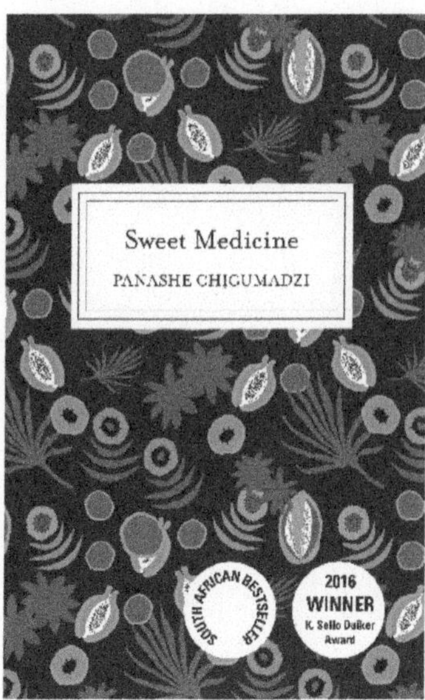